VALLEY OF SKULLS

Fargo was after two things: a priceless cannon and a beautiful woman. But the only way to the Valley of the Skulls was through land so primitive that word of revolution would not have reached it. There was a reward out for him in Guatemala and there were the bandits in Yucatan, and they would have stalked him all the way, if they did not kill him for his guns and outfit first . . .

JOHN BENTEEN

♦

FARGO: VALLEY OF SKULLS

Complete and Unabridged

LINFORD
Leicester

First published in the U.S.A.

First Linford Edition
published July 1991

British Library CIP Data

Benteen, John
    Fargo: Valley of Skulls. — Large print ed. —
Linford western library
I. Title
823.914

ISBN 0–7089–7033–8

Published by
F. A. Thorpe (Publishing) Ltd.
Anstey, Leicestershire
Set by Words & Graphics Ltd.
Anstey, Leicestershire
Printed and bound in Great Britain by
T. J. Press (Padstow) Ltd., Padstow, Cornwall

1

THEY were killing machines, the two fighting cocks. Hatched and bred with only one objective, one destiny: combat.

The men, nearly fifty of them, made a circle behind the warehouse on the outskirts of San Antonio. The sun was hot, the air still; in the distance church bells tolled. The men shouted, waved handfuls of money, betting. Inside the circle, the handlers 'billed' their chickens: two barefooted Mexicans moved close to one another so the gamefowl could slash at each other with the beaks of snakelike heads. Then the referee, a businessman of the town in white shirt and tie, said loudly, "Pit!"

A circle had been drawn in the dust. The handlers moved to opposite sides, lowered their roosters to the ground. Then they released them. The two birds

1

charged at one another, hackles raised, the steel spurs, razor-sharp, strapped to their feet, gleaming. In a flurry of glittering feathers, wings beating, heads lashing, gaffs slashing, they met, left the ground, fell back.

On the circle's inside edge, Fargo crouched, watching closely. One cock was bronze and gold; his money rode on it. The other was gun-metal blue. Now, as the birds hit the dust, he sucked in breath. The bronze cock was underneath, the blue on top — and the blue had both spurs sunk deep into the bronze one's breast and belly.

The bronze cock's wings beat, hard, desperately. "Handle," the referee said.

The two men moved in. Carefully, the bronze cock's owner detached the blue cock's gaffs from flesh. He picked up the bronze one, blood dribbling between his fingers. There was blood on its head, too, and in its eyes. As he moved back to the circle's edge, he used his tongue to lick, delicately, the rooster's eyes clean.

"Pit," the referee said.

The blue cock, unharmed, charged. The bronze cock, dying, shoved its way forward awkwardly. It would fight to the last beat of its heart, be dangerous so long as one flicker of life remained. Fargo felt a kinship with the bird. It was doomed, yes, but it was going out the way a creature bred to fight should; the way he would go out when his time came. Around him the crowd's shouting rose to crescendo, but he was silent. For him there was meaning, significance, in the bronze cock's lethal determination to deal damage before it died.

Trailing blood, it pushed itself into ring's center with faltering wings and limber legs. The blue rooster hit it hard, confidently, knocked it on its back, slashed at it with its gaffs. The bronze cock beat the dust with wings, slashed back, and found a target for its gaffs in the blue one's exposed breast. Suddenly the blue cock went into convulsions. Wings flapping wildly, it rolled and twisted, dragging the bronze one with it, spurs locked deep in flesh. Then the blue cock was underneath; all at once it went wholly limp. Fastened on top of it, the bronze one looked around with glittering eyes beginning to glaze. The referee moved in, closely. The blue cock was motionless, dead. The bronze one beat its wings again, tried to rise on the body of its opponent, threw back its bloody head and golden neck. From its throat came one feeble half-crow of triumph. Then it too went into the wing-flapping convulsions of death, fell forward, and was still.

The referee stood up, faced the crowd. "The red cock wins. Next bird."

Fargo's mouth twisted in a faint grin of satisfaction. He straightened, gray eyes searching the crowd. Where was Galloway?

Then he saw him, striding away quickly down the alley between the warehouses. Fargo's lips thinned; he grunted a curse, shoved through the mob, went after him. As he moved with long-legged stride, his polished cavalry boots struck the dusty earth sharply, and Galloway could not have helped hearing him come, but Galloway did not look back.

Fargo quickened his pace. He was a big man, well over six feet, broad in the shoulder, heavy in the chest, narrow in waist and hips. An old cavalry hat topped a short-cropped thatch of hair gone prematurely snow-white above a face hard, craggy, marked at the age of thirty-five by years of tough outdoor living. His features were ugly, brutal, yet somehow attractive in their ruthless strength. He wore a white shirt, a tie, a corduroy jacket especially cut to conceal the holstered Colt .38 Officer's Model revolver under his left arm, whipcord pants, and boots. He could have been a prosperous cattleman or an oil wildcatter. He had been both in his time, but now he was a soldier of fortune, a man who hired out to fight no matter what the odds — provided the money was right. He was good at his trade and he did not come cheap; he liked money.

And Galloway owed him some. Fargo's long legs closed the gap between them.

Then he barked, harshly: "Galloway!"

The other did not halt. Indeed, appearing not to hear, he moved on faster.

"All right," Fargo said, to no one in particular. Then he ran.

He ran the way a panther travels, in graceful, fluid bounds that covered ground with deceptive swiftness. Galloway heard him coming, seemed about to break, then thought better of it. At last he halted, turned, a man in a big sombrero, suit, tie, and high heeled boots. As tall as Fargo, he was a few years older, with a rocky slab of a face, huge hands doubling now to fists, and a barrel chest. He was, he claimed, a cattle buyer. Maybe, Fargo thought as he faced Galloway, he was also a welcher. In Fargo's book, there was nothing lower.

Galloway's face was pale beneath its tan; his black eyes narrowed. "You called me, Fargo?"

"Yeah." Fargo halted five feet away. "There's a little matter of a thousand bucks you owe me. The red cock won."

"No. They killed each other." Galloway

6

shook his head. "All bets off."

"If you don't know cockfightin', Galloway, you shouldn't risk money on it. The last bird alive is the winner." He grinned, not pleasantly, but like a hungry wolf spotting prey. "Let's have the *dinero*, Galloway."

Galloway's eyes batted. Then he smiled. "Okay, sure. If that's the way it works." He reached in his coat pocket, and his hand came out holding a snubnosed, nickel-plated .32

He was fast, but Neal Fargo made him look slow and stupid. No man reached like that without triggering reflexes in Fargo's body, and his boot was already coming up. It connected, and Galloway squalled, and in the same instant Fargo moved in and his big hand caught the other's wrist. Fargo squeezed, and bones slid and ground together in his grasp, and the pistol dropped. Fargo brought his right across, hard; slammed the doubled-over Galloway back against the warehouse wall. Then he kicked the gun and sent it skittering down the alley as Galloway, groaning, dropped to his knees.

"I'll have the thousand," Fargo said, standing over him.

Galloway sucked in breath. Then, without warning, he launched himself at Fargo.

He came up fast, and his big head, cannonball solid, caught Fargo in the belly, knocked him across the alley and against the warehouse on the right. Galloway came after him, fast, but not fast enough. Fargo dropped low, and Galloway's double-fisted, clubbing blow missed and Fargo drove his own fist deep in the other's belly and, simultaneously, chopped Galloway across the back of the neck with the blade of his left hand.

Galloway slammed against the wall, then sagged. On his knees, he tried weakly to seize Fargo's ankles. Fargo stepped aside, kicked him in the chin. Galloway sprawled, rolled over on his back. Not quite out, he shook his head groggily.

"Get up," said Fargo from above him.

"Get up and pay off." He pulled the Colt from its shoulder holster. "Or next time you git a pistol whippin' that'll make you look like you tried to kiss a bobcat. Up, Galloway."

Groaning, Galloway struggled to his knees. Then he pushed himself to his feet, stood there swaying. "For God's sake, Fargo," he husked, "don't hit me again." He reached in his coat once more, this time brought out a wallet. His hands shook as he counted out the money.

Fargo took it, still holding the gun trained. He counted it swiftly, accurately, thrust it in his own coat. Then he backed away, picked up the nickel-plated gun, jacked the cartridges out, stuck them in his pocket, and dropped the weapon in the dust.

His eyes locked Galloway's. "Don't you come around me again, you cheap bastard," he said coldly. "Don't you come around me as long as I'm in San Antone, you hear?" Then he turned contemptuously and walked away.

Behind him, Galloway made a strange

sobbing sound, as if he were crying over the loss of his money.

Fargo lost fifteen hundred on the next fight, won two thousand on the one after that. Then it was over; the crowd broke up. Fargo walked through the warehouses to the street and caught a trolley uptown.

He was staying in the best hotel. Women in the lobby followed the tall, hard-faced, ugly man with their eyes as he passed through.

His room was large. He peeled off coat and tie, turned on the electric fan. He did not remove the shoulder-holstered gun. There was a bottle of whiskey on the bureau. He pulled its cork with strong teeth, drank long and deep then put it aside.

Turning, he pulled from beneath the bed a large, brassbound trunk with a heavy padlock. He unfastened it, took most of his winnings from his coat, was about to deposit the cash inside. But he could not resist the guns; and, one by one, he took them out and checked them.

He was a professional and they were the tools of his trade. Like all master craftsmen, he respected his tools and kept them in meticulous working order.

First there was the .30-30 Winchester Model 94 carbine. He took that out of its scabbard, checked its oil, worked its lever. Satisfied, he laid it aside.

Something glowed in his eyes as he lifted out the next item. A case of finest chamois skin was stripped away to reveal a double-barreled sawed-off shotgun, a Fox Sterlingworth, ten-gauge, its breech beautifully chased and engraved. He ran his thumb over the inscription worked into the decoration: *To Neal Fargo, gratefully, from T. Roosevelt.* His mouth quirked. It had been a long time since he had heard from the man he'd served in the rough Riders in Cuba. He wondered what the tough old coot was up to. Probably hunting lions somewhere in Africa or jaguars in South America.

Originally a fowling piece, the gun's

short barrels were now open bore, each capable of throwing nine chilled buckshot in a deadly pattern from which, at close range, nothing could escape. Fargo had attached a sling to it, and now he slipped his arm through it and let the gun hang muzzles down behind his back. Then he hooked his right thumb in the sling, twitched. As if by magic, the two short barrels whisked up under his armpit, pointed straight ahead; in the same clocktick of time, Fargo's left hand shot across his body, tripped both triggers. The gun clicked twice. In that position, it was upside down, but that would have made no difference at all if it had been loaded; not to anyone standing in front of it.

Fargo smiled faintly, transferred the gun to his other shoulder, went through the same routine. He had been born ambidextrous. It was a knack that had saved his life more than once.

He checked the shotgun carefully for oil and cleanliness, then restored it to the chamois case. He put it aside, took out the Batangas knife.

Twin handles of water-buffalo horn folded forward, sheathed the blade. Fargo flicked a catch, jerked his wrist; both handles opened, snapping back into his palm, revealing ten inches of the hardest, sharpest, best-crafted blade a knife-fighter could obtain. This weapon had come from Batangas on Luzon, where Fargo had served a hitch in the cavalry during the Philippine Insurrection; and the boast of its owner that it could be driven through a silver dollar with a single blow without breaking or dulling had been proved by him. Fargo was an expert with it, and he made two quick practice passes, blade low and parallel with the ground, then flipped the handles back around it, locked them, and restored the weapon to its special sheath. He laid it aside, pulled out the bandoliers.

There were two big ones to criss-cross over his chest; one glittered with ammo for the Winchester; the other held fifty shells for the shotgun. All its loops were full. He put them aside, too, and pulled out the cartridge belt and pistol holster he wore around his waist when he was not in town. Fat cartridges winked at him, their gray noses hollow inside; these were dum-dums, designed to expand explosively on impact, possessing awful stopping power and capable of doing dreadful things to flesh. They were not pleasant in their effect, but when Fargo shot a man, he wanted him to stay down.

The trunk also contained clothes suitable for different climates; Fargo had plied his trade of professional soldier, hired gunman, and revolutionist in many parts of the world. He'd had other occupations, too: born on a New Mexican ranch, his parents killed by Apaches, he had run away from his foster home at the age of twelve. Since then, he'd fought in Cuba, punched cows, logged big timber, wildcatted in the oil fields, boxed in the prize ring, gambled as a professional, and once, when down on his luck, had even served a term as bouncer in a whorehouse.

In addition to the clothes, there were boxes of spare ammunition and reloading tools and primers. Fargo was fussy about his ammunition; he wanted certain powder loads and bullet weights, and when he could not buy them, he put them together himself.

There was also five thousand in gold in the trunk, all that was left of ten that he had brought back across the river a week ago. He made money fast and spent it the same way. Now he added the winnings from the cockfight, restored the weapons carefully to the trunk, and put the trunk back under the bed. Then, as he was having another drink, someone knocked on the door.

Instinctively, Fargo's hand went to the gun. "Who is it?"

The woman's voice was low. "Carla, Fargo."

He grinned, opened the door quickly. She came in just as quickly and shut it softly behind her. She was tall, fullbreasted, her hair black as a raven's wing, her eyes huge and lustrous. Her waist was slim, her hips curved beneath the clinging dress; although the garment masked them. He knew how long, how superb her legs were. She was one of the reasons he spent money so fast.

"Neal," she whispered, and she came to him. He felt the soft cushions of her breasts against his chest, her nails digging into his back, her lips opening beneath his mouth as he held her and kissed her. The kiss lasted a long time; when it was over, her eyes were shining, her breasts heaving, and she was panting slightly.

That grin came back on Fargo's face. "Where is he this afternoon?"

"Bert? He left for Marfa to buy some cattle after Sunday dinner." Her voice was husky. "We've got the whole night ahead of us, Neal."

Then she turned around. "Unbutton me," she said.

Fargo did.

He had met Carla Reeves in the hotel lobby two days before. She had just come out of the dining room with several other well-dressed women, the wives, Fargo tagged them, of San Antonio's upper crust. She was the loveliest and most expensive-looking of them all. For an instant, their eyes had met. That had done it. When he came out of the dining room, she had let the others go on without her and she was waiting in the lobby . . .

Her husband was fifteen years older than she, and he dealt in cattle and land; it kept him traveling. That made it easier. Not that his presence in town would have stopped Fargo. When he saw something he wanted, he took it. If a man couldn't see to his own wife, that was his tough luck.

Now he ran his eyes over Carla's nakedness as she finished stripping off her clothes. He liked the way the big breasts, nipples hard as rocks, stood out firmly; he liked the white velvet softness of her belly, the long, soft-thighed, yet strong legs. He liked the full, lush mouth. But, he thought, it was about time to end this. Might as well wind it up today.

"Aren't you going to undress?" she whispered.

"Sure." He stripped off the gunbelt, pulled off his shirt. Her eyes were hungry, admiring, as they ranged the tanned, muscular torso scarred and puckered with old wounds. Then the boots and the rest of the clothes. By then, she was on the bed waiting. He went to her.

When it was over, Fargo got out of bed, lit a cigarette, took a pull at the bottle, passed it to her.

She drank from it like a man, gave it back, looked at him with lambent eyes. "Fargo . . ."

"Yeah."

"I've been thinking . . . If I told Bert, he'd give me a divorce . . ."

Fargo took his cigarette from his mouth, blew smoke. "I wouldn't do a thing like that, Carla."

Her eyes widened, face paled. She hitched up in bed, instinctively throwing the sheet across her loins. "What do you mean?" she whispered.

"Well, it's time for me to be moving on," he said.

"Moving on? Neal — "

"Ease off, Carla." He smiled faintly. "You came into this with your eyes wide open. I never said anything to change that."

"B-but I thought, I hoped — "

"That you could tame me down and keep me here?"

"No. No — that I . . . we . . . the two of us, could stay together. That you'd take me with you when you went . . . "

Fargo shrugged, took the bottle, drank again. "No dice, Carla. Where I go, I travel alone. A woman wouldn't last a minute in some of the messes I get into, and neither would I if I had one to look out for. No. No, you stay with Bert. He's nice and steady and a little bit dumb. He knows how to get hold of a dollar without havin' to lay his life on the line to do it. You'll be a lot better off with him . . . "

Carla swallowed hard; tears sprang into her eyes. "Neal, please — "

He shook his head, wordlessly.

She was silent for a moment. Then she said, "Well, at least we'll have a few more days together."

"I'm afraid not," Fargo said. He reached for the bottle one more time. "I'll be movin' on, Carla. I've stayed put too long already. Two weeks in San Antone, eatin', drinkin', and — " He looked at her and grinned. "That's about as long as I can take the peaceful life. I got to head out again, scratch up a job."

"Where will you go?" Her voice was a whisper.

"Don't you read the papers? Madero, president of Mexico — he's just been assassinated. That means more revolution down yonder. Revolutions mean money for a fightin' man. I'll likely haul freight soon. Meanwhile, I've got to get everything in shape. So . . . This is the end of it. Today."

She stared at him. She read the seriousness of what he had said on that ugly, rock-hard face. Not a stupid woman, she accepted that this was indeed the end of it, that no protest she could make would change it. She drew in a long breath that made her breasts rise. "All right," she said at last, dully. "If this is the end of it, it's the end of it. But . . . I don't have to leave right now, do I?"

Fargo looked back at her and grinned.

"No," he said, and he moved toward the bed again.

2

SHE was a smart woman, Fargo thought; she could accept the inevitable and had managed not to cry. When she had gone, a trace of her perfume lingered in the room. He dressed slowly, had another drink. He had meant what he said. He had been in town too long; he was getting soft and flabby. Everything in him cried out for action, combat. He was, he told himself, too much like that bronze rooster — and, undoubtedly, he would end up the same way someday in some godforsaken corner of the world. But for the chicken, it had been better than having its neck wrung in a barnyard to make Sunday dinner for some fat *paisano*; for a man, that kind of death was better than the one in bed — slow, lingering, hanging on to life when life was useless. He slipped the colt into its scabbard, adjusted it carefully beneath his arm, put on his jacket and left the room. The way to die was with your spurs deep in the enemy.

Now, he thought, he'd head down to Mex Town, range the cantinas there, pick up what information he could about events across the border. If battle flared between all the contending factions after Madero's death, gun-running should be profitable . . .

He passed through the lobby, out the door, onto the sidewalk.

He turned right, strode along, not faltering, giving no sign that he had just realized he was being followed.

But they had, he knew, been waiting for him in the lobby. Now they had come out on the street, too, not far behind. As he walked along, they stood indecisively by the hotel entrance, giving him a chance to widen the gap between them. He saw them in the slanted plateglass window of a store, heads close together, muttering to one another. He knew who they were immediately, those two, thick-bodied men in business suits and Eastern hats. Pinkertons: detectives.

Fargo smiled faintly. Pinkerton was hiring an inferior breed of agents these days. He walked on until they fell in a hundred yards behind him. There were not many people on the street at this time Sunday night. They came slowly, tentatively, pretending to be strolling, looking into store windows.

He teased them along like that until he had walked the long way down into Mex Town. Here the buildings were of adobe, and there were no street lights. Torches flared on corners where sidewalk vendors had their carts; mangy dogs ranged the gutters. There was guitar music, the sound of voices singing the sad love songs of Coahuila and Leon. The Pinkertons had moved in closer now, as if afraid theyd lose him. Fargo turned into a cantina, pushed through its swinging doors.

It was a grubby place, with a dirt floor, a rude bar, a few tables; it was lamplit, and what patrons there were seemed shabby. A few beat-up girls moved among them, listlessly. Fargo found a vacant table where he could sit with his back to the wall, eased his big frame into a chair, ordered tequila. The barman brought the bottle, a plate of quartered limes, and salt. Fargo went through the routine with salt and lime and the sharp, raw alcohol, leaned back, waited, aware of the curious eyes on this big gringo in the army hat who had ordered what he wanted in perfect border dialect.

In a minute, now, the Pinkertons would have to come in. They would be at a disadvantage, facing him in the sort of place neither was used to. Wondered again why the agency was trailing him with Easterners. They stood out like sore thumbs.

Then he saw their fedoras above the batwing doors. Hesitantly, almost reluctantly, they pushed in. They could have been twins; short, but powerful of body, pale faces thickly mustached. They stood blinking inside the door; then they saw Fargo.

He raised a big, scarred hand. "Hey, you fellas. Come over, sit. I'll buy a drink."

They hesitated, looking at one another. Fargo's wolf grin spread across his face. "Come on, it's on me."

One said something to his companion. Then they came to his table. The one on the right had a black moustache; the other had a red one. Red Mustache said, "Much obliged."

They sat down. Fargo called in dialect for two more glasses. Then he looked directly at him. "You damned private dicks always do things the hard way. You want to talk to me, why didn't you stop me in the lobby?"

Their faces paled. They stared at one another.

"Goddamn it," Fargo said. "Don't you think I know Pinkerton agents when I see 'em?" Suddenly his good humor vanished. "What the hell are you doin' on my trail? I don't have any rap against me. Who sent you?"

Black Mustache licked his lips. "All

right," he said. "All right, don't get your back up. You're Neal Fargo?"

"You know confounded well who I am."

"We wanted to be sure." Red Mustache had the deeper voice; he was obviously the leader. "Another thing, we didn't want anybody seeing us talk together."

"Talk about what?"

Red Mustache cleared his throat. "My name's Dolan. This is Torrence. We were sent here to look you up and make you a proposition."

"What kind of proposition?"

Dolan's dark eyes flickered. "I don't know. All I know is that somebody wants you in New York City. It's our job to take you there."

Fargo sat up straight. "Take me?"

"We mean, escort you," Torrence said hastily. "Look, Mr. Fargo. Somebody in New York — I don't know who, neither does Dolan — hired the agency to find you and ask you to come to New York, all expenses paid. We were told to promise you that it would be worth your while if you went."

"Worth my while," said Fargo. "What do you mean 'worth my while?' "

"There's money in it for you," Dolan said, "A lot of money."

Fargo looked at him sardonically. "That a fact? How much did whoever this is send with you to pay down?"

Torrence blinked, chewed his mustache. "We're to pay your way, all expenses, to New York City."

Fargo laughed softly. "That all?"

"All we're authorized to do."

"Sorry, gentlemen. I ain't lost nothing in New York. My time's valuable, and I don't have a couple of weeks to spend traveling back and forth on a wild goose chase. You got some deal you want to put up to me, put it. And lay some money on the table when you do. That's the way I work."

"We don't have anything to lay on the table," Dolan said. "All we're authorized to do is find you and get you to New York."

Fargo's mouth twisted. He took a

brown cigarette from a pack, thrust it between good white teeth, scratched a match with this thumbnail, lit it. He blew the strong smoke at them. "I don't go nowhere with no money down. I got to have the cash in front; that's the way I work."

"You'll get it in New York."

"I don't know that."

"You will, we're authorized to promise that."

His twisted mouth warped itself farther into that terrible grin. "Promises? Pinkerton promises especially? A Pinkerton would sell out his own grandmother without flappin' an eyelash if he thought it would help him on a case."

Dolan sucked in a deep breath. Then he leaned forward across the table. "Look, Mr. Fargo, they don't tell us a whole lot, except what we're supposed to do — no questions asked, it's our job. But I can say this to you. There is a very powerful man who wants you in New York. He might just be the most powerful man in the whole United States. One thing's damn sure, he's just about the richest." He hesitated. "I understand, off the record, he's the one who hired the agency to round you up. He wants to see you, size you up, and if he likes the cut of your jib, he'll tell you the rest himself."

"And if he don't, I'll have wasted maybe two valuable weeks when I could have been turning a little profit on my own." Fargo's voice roughened. "I told you, God damn it, I don't work in the blind. I don't know who this joker is that hired you, and I don't give a hoot. If he's got so much money, let him lay it out, then I'll talk to him. But put it up in front; that's the only way I deal."

They were silent for a moment. Then Dolan said heavily, reluctantly, "Mr. Fargo, he has a job for a fighting man. He can afford the best there is, and that's supposed to be you. But he didn't get rich by dealing in the blind either; he wants to see you face to face before he lays out the cash. And I'll tell you now, if you cross this man, you're in bad trouble. He don't like to be crossed, and the man that does it to him, well, this country ain't big enough to hold him."

Fargo blew pale smoke. "Dolan, you threatenin' me?"

"Telling you," said Dolan. "Our job is to find you and bring you to New York."

"Even if I don't want to go?"

"Even," Dolan said, "if you don't want to go."

Fargo snorted softly. His eyes shuttled back and forth from one of them to the other. He raised his hand slightly, in position for a shoulder draw. "The two of you?"

"No," said Dolan. "The eight of us. This man doesn't play small, Fargo. Besides, there're six more Pinkerton agents here in San Antonio to make sure we bring you in. I think, one way or another, we can do the job."

Fargo was silent for a moment. Then he said, "I don't go anywhere I don't choose to. You'll lose some Pinkertons, Dolan."

"That's part of the game," Dolan said. "You can't fight us all."

Torrence put in, voice placatory, "Mr. Fargo. Why stir up a fuss? There's money in it for you, we've promised you that. We don't want to have to use force. But if we have to, we will."

"Eight Pinkerton agents," Fargo said thoughtfully. "This *is* a high mogul, ain't it? I don't suppose it occurred to him that if he had sent me the cash he's spending on you people, I would have come right away."

"That's not the point of it," Dolan began.

"It is to me," said Fargo. "I've already found out how this guy who hired you operates and I don't like it a damned bit. He may be the most powerful man in the United States, but maybe I am the most independent. I never met but one man in this country yet that I would run to when he snapped his fingers. I served under him in Cuba. He got to be President after a while, and he was pretty powerful himself. Sorry, you guys, but your big operator don't impress me a damn bit. If he wants me to gamble two weeks of my time, you tell him to lay about five thousand dollars on the table and I'll consider it."

"Mr. Fargo," Torrence said sadly. "You'll make us resort to force."

"No," said Fargo easily. "You make me do that." In the same instant, he kneed over the table and it slammed into the two men and knocked them backwards. His hand whisked to the Colt and pulled it out. They sprawled on the floor. The laughter and chatter in the cantina broke off, and Fargo stood over them, menacing them with the gun.

"It's loaded with hollow points," he said. "They make an awful hole in a fellar's head. Lie still, because if you don't, Pinkerton's gonna be short two men."

Fargo backed away, holstering the colt. "All right, you two greenhorns. Up and on your feet. Now, you can go off and round up your other six and lose some men, or you can go send a telegram.

Bring me five thousand hard cash and a ticket to New York and I'll go see your boss man. But don't you come after me again talkin' about *making* me go anywhere unless you want to lose some blood. You got it?"

They stared up at him with frightened eyes. He threw a gold piece on the bar and stalked out as they scrambled to their feet. He went quickly, alertly, back to the hotel, but they did not follow him and there was no more trouble.

Eighteen hours later, the two of them appeared again. This time, they knocked at the door of his room.

When he opened it, the first thing they did, hastily, as if afraid, was to pass over a sheaf of fifty one hundred dollar bills.

It was an enormous brownstone on lower Fifth Avenue. A liveried butler answered Fargo's ring, and his eyes widened at the sight of the sweat-and-weather-stained campaign hat, jaunty and disreputable on the side of Fargo's white-thatched head.

"I'm Neal Fargo. Your boss is expecting me."

"Oh. Oh, yes, sir. Come in, please, sir. I . . . I'll let the master know you're here. Shall I take your hat?"

"No," said Fargo.

The butler vanished. He stood there looking around the foyer.

Money. You could see it, touch it, smell it in the furnishings of the place. Oil money, railroad money. Fargo's mouth twisted. The Pinkerton agents hadn't exaggerated. Ned D. Stoneman was probably the richest man in the United States. Maybe the most powerful, too, for his billions could buy Congressmen, Senators, Governors — even Presidents. He had got those billons by being totally, completely ruthless, by ruining his competitors without mercy, buying only what he couldn't steal or grab. He was old now, in his seventies, Fargo guessed; but according to the papers, his rapacity had not diminished one bit. He had more money than he could spend if he lived to be two thousand, and

35

still he clutched for more. His railroad empire webbed the whole Northeast; his oil empire encompassed Oklahoma, Texas, and Pennsylvania. He would, Fargo thought, be interesting to deal with.

Then the butler reappeared. "Mr. Stoneman will see you within the hour, sir."

"Will he?"

"Yes, sir."

"You tell Mr. Stoneman that he will see me within the next five minutes or he won't see me at all."

The butler looked shocked. "But, sir."

"Get your ass in gear," said Fargo. "And tell him that."

"Yes, sir!" Pale-faced, as if doomed to human sacrifice, the butler vanished again. Two minutes later he reappeared, slightly dazed. "Mr. Stoneman will see you now."

"I figured he would," Fargo said, and followed the man up the stairs.

On the second floor, he entered a corridor faced with many doors, crowded with curious objects on pedestals and in alcoves. His eyes ranged over them with interest; he had seen their like in Mexico. Idols and carvings: Aztec, Toltec, Mayan, Olmec: apparently the old man had a craving for Mexican prehistoric art. Then the butler rapped on double doors with a carved bronze knocker.

"Come in," a thin, dry voice said irritably from behind them.

The butler opened the door and announced: "Mr. Neal Fargo."

Fargo entered. The room was huge, high ceilinged, and it had a reek in it like the effluvium from a rotten tooth. That reek could only have come from the old man behind the desk before the huge Italian marble fireplace.

He sat there, motionless, the only things alive in his gaunt and withered face the two blue eyes, cold and blue as chips of ice. His head was nearly bald, save for two or three greasy strands of limp hair laid across it at random — his cheeks sunken, his mouth puckered with toothlessness — too cheap, Fargo guessed, even for dentistry to save his teeth. His nose was the most striking thing about him . . . enormous, curved and hooked like a hawk's bill. "Mr. Fargo," he said. "Welcome." A handful of dead leaves, crumpled in a fist, would have produced exactly the same dry, whispering, rasping tone.

"Hello, Mr. Stoneman," Fargo said.

Stoneman arose, slowly. He wore a cheap, almost threadbare suit, and it hung on his gaunt frame like a bag. Slowly, reluctantly, he put out a hand that was a withered claw. Fargo touched it briefly, but its cold waxen texture was not pleasant, and he took his own hand away at once.

"Sit down, Mr. Fargo."

"Yes. Thank you." Fargo pulled up a carved chair before the desk and sat. He still wore the Colt under his jacket. Stoneman lowered himself behind the desk again.

"Look around, Mr. Fargo."

Fargo accepted the invitation. He

surveyed the room with the wariness of a hunted animal, although he had already sized it up upon entry. It was full of the same sort of objects that clogged the hall: more of the ancient Indian carvings of Mexico. In addition, there were suits or armor which Fargo recognized as ancient Spanish.

"What do you see, sir?" the dry, crackling voice inquired.

"You're interested in the old-time Indians."

"Of Mexico and Central America, yes. I . . . understand you know those regions well."

"I've fought in revolutions all through them. Not always on the winning side."

"Oh? That discourages me. A man should always be on the winning side."

"I disagree. Losing once in a while keeps a man's skin loose and his blood running."

"Your philosophy, not mine. Well, that makes no difference now. You drive a hard bargain, Mr. Fargo."

"Next time you want me, just send

money, not detectives. It makes things easier."

The puckered mouth, not unlike the opening of a drawstringed bag, built a parody of a smile. "That is more in the line of my own philosophy. We will understand each other."

"Maybe," Fargo said. "All right, Mr. Stoneman, let's cut out the rigmarole. You paid five thousand to bring me here. For that you get an hour. Maybe you'd like to get to the point."

"Yes. I'll do that. My own time is worth something like three thousand dollars and hour. Yours seems to come higher. All right, Mr. Fargo, I have checked carefully. You are the best freelance fighting man available, despite your price. Also, you know lower Mexico and Central America. Have you ever been in the Mexican state of Chiapas?"

"Once. There's not much there. It's the farthest south in Mexico, slam up against Guatemala. A few little towns, a hell of a big rain forest. If you get far enough in the jungle, some old Indian ruins."

"Old Indian ruins. Aye, indeed." The withered man gestured. "Mr. Fargo. In that rain forest lies the cradle of one of the earlest civilizations of America — the Mayas."

"Sure," said Fargo. "I noticed you had some Mayan carvings here."

"You know the Maya then?"

Fargo took out a thin, black cigar, bit off its end, thrust it between his teeth. "There's not much anybody knows about the Maya. They were one of the oldest, earliest Indian civilizations on the continent. They built pyramids and temples and big cities and then they got rubbed out, just before the Spanish came. Something was left of them but the Spanish wiped out even that remnant. But at one time, they were the rulers of southern Mexico and Guatemala. There are still some Maya Indians down there. They speak the bastard dialect, but they've forgot all the old secrets of their ancestors."

"Good." The old man almost smiled. "A very concise summary. I'm glad you won't need a lot of background." He leaned back in his chair. "Mr. Fargo, in my younger days, long before you were born, I was a man much like yourself. A soldier of fortune — a *filibustero*, if you please — roaming all that country, fighting here, there, wherever. Well, those days are long past, but my memory of them is not. I became fascinated with Mexico — with its art, with its history. Now I am very rich and I can afford to indulge that interest. I have smuggled out of Mexico every important prehistoric statue or *stela* — that's a carved stone monument — or *objet d'art* that money can buy. I am fascinated by the secrets of the Maya, the Aztec, the other ancient tribes."

"It's interesting as hell, I'll admit," Fargo said.

"And profitable." The old man's eyes gleamed. "Someday all these things will be worth their weight in platinum."

"That's what makes it interesting to you," Fargo said.

"Of course."

"Where do I come in?"

Stoneman leaned forward, propping his elbows on his desk. "Have you ever heard of the Valley of Skulls?"

"No," said Fargo.

"Not surprising. It's deep in the Lacándon Forest, that vast tropical rain forest between Chiapas and Guatemala. No one else knows of it, either, except myself, Dr. Telford of the Smithsonian Institute, and my son, Ned, Jr." He hesitated. "And the members of their expedition, of course."

"What expedition?" Fargo blew cigar smoke.

"I'll come to the point quickly. Dr. Telford is an archeologist, a specialist in the ancient civilizations of Southern Mexico and Central America. Six months ago he returned from Madrid where he had been doing research in the Royal Spanish Library. Do you know what a codex is, Fargo?"

"No."

"The Maya had books. A codex is their form of book, a strip of parchment, inscribed by their priests, folded between wooden covers. The Spanish friars, anxious to stamp out all elements of pagan religion, burned all they could get their hands on. But a few survived. Dr. Nelson Telford discovered one in the Madrid Library, along with a Spanish interpretation, anonymous, that must have been made by a Spaniard who had learned the ancient Maya picture writing."

Fargo arched a brow. "So?"

"This codex told of a place in the Lacándon Forest called the Valley of Skulls. It was a sacred Mayan place, supposedly with an enormous temple. Human sacrifice was practiced. In that valley the skulls of the victims throughout the Mayan empire — and it was a vast, enormous empire, Fargo — all the sacrificial bones and skulls were brought together in a single temple. It was the most sacred place of the whole Mayan civilization." He broke off, as if so much talking had exhausted him. Then he continued after a couple of deep breaths.

"Knowing my interest in the ancient civilizations, Dr. Telford came to me. After he had presented his findings, I agreed to finance an expedition to the Valley of Skulls. Well, I have done that. They are there right now, digging. My son, Ned, is with them to protect my interests . . . You see, Mr. Fargo, I make first claim on anything of value they may discover."

"What they excavate belongs to Mexico," Fargo said.

"Not if I can get it out. And in Mexico, money can accomplish anything." The old eyes gleamed. "Before I'm through, I'll have the most magnificent collection of prehistoric art and statuary in the world, Fargo — and the most valuable! That's why I sent Ned with the expedition! He's a chip off the old block; he can manage anything."

"In that case, where do I come in?"

Stoneman cleared his throat, a grating, phlegmy sound. "Ned is clever. He is a good fighting man, too. I used to be, and I have taught him all I know. Everything was in order until President Madero was killed. Now Mexico will lapse back into chaos, anarchy. It will be every man for himself for years — bandits, soldiers, the like. I know the drill. I used to fight down there." Suddenly, shakily, he arose, went to the mantel, pulled down a map above it. His hand trembled as he pointed out places. "The expedition is trapped, Fargo. Behind them, to the north, the revolutionary forces. Ahead of them, to the south, that huge rain forest. Dr. Telford, his daughter, their assistants, and Ned are penned up in the Valley of Skulls and they can't move. They can't come out the way they went in because of the revolution. They can't go out the other way because of the rain forest; they'd never make it through there. They can't move to the Atlantic Coast or the Pacific because of soldiers and bandits, not without risking . . ." He hesitated.

"Risking what?" Fargo asked. He had caught that undertone in Stoneman's voice.

"Something rare. Rare beyond all

imagining, and priceless." The withered lips curved. "Something worth its weight in gold."

"What?" Fargo asked.

"That need not concern you," Stoneman said. "If you accept this job, you'll know soon enough. Anyway, Fargo, what I want you to do is to go to the Valley of Skulls in Chiapas, and somehow help the expedition fight its way out — along with anything Ned deems valuable enough to bring out with it."

3

FOR a moment, the vast room, with its brooding sculptures of thick-bodied, ancient Indians long dead, was silent.

Then Fargo said, "That's a tall order. Every bandit and every outlaw in lower Mexico will be on the prod now that the government's collapsed. They'll block your expedition off. And the Lacándon Forest. Nobody gets through there."

"That's your problem," Stoneman said. "I paid you five thousand dollars to come here. I'll pay you another five to go there. You bring them out, the people and the things my son designates as baggage, you'll get another five."

Fargo laughed.

"What's so funny?" Stoneman asked, frowning.

"You want me to work my way through revolutionaries, bandits, jungle, whatever

— rescue some scientists — not only that, maybe haul out tons of stuff, fighting all the way and you offer fifteen thousand?"

"This day and time that's a substantial sum."

"Maybe to you. I can make more than that in a month running guns."

"Mr. Fargo. You're a hard man to deal with. All right, twenty then. But you'll be under Ned's orders from the time you make contact with him."

Fargo stood up. "I enjoyed the conversation, Mr. Stoneman." He turned as if to go. At that moment, the double doors of the room opened; only later did he realize that Stoneman had pushed a buzzer on his desk. Then, though, Fargo halted, staring at the three bulky Irish plug-uglies who barred his exit.

"I don't do business this way, Stoneman," he said thinly. "But I may kill some men before I get out on the street."

"They're experienced. They may kill you too."

"I'll take that chance."

He stood there, hand inside his coat.

"Mr. Fargo, I don't like the way you deal," Stoneman quavered. "I have a gun pointed at your back."

"You couldn't hit me with it," Fargo said easily. "I've seen how your hand shakes. You're too old." He grinned. "I could kill you and maybe all three of them. Then I would have to go to the Colonel for protection. But he'd stand by me."

"The Colonel?"

"I was in the Rough Riders in Cuba; he commanded 'em."

He did not take his eyes off the three men at the door, but he heard Stoneman sigh at the mention of that name. "The Colonel. Yes. He's my worst enemy, my most powerful one. I've heard mention of your connection with him."

"Then tell your men to get out of the way," said Fargo. "We can't deal."

For a moment, the old man was silent. "Fargo," he said at last. "Ten when you leave. Twenty when you get back. Add that to the five you've already got, it makes thirty-five thousand."

Fargo stood rigidly, hand on gun butt. "Fifteen when I leave."

"Forty thousand total?" Stoneman's voice quavered.

"Take it or leave it," said Fargo. "Because in thirty seconds I'm walking out of here. If your people get in my way, you'd better be prepared to pay their funeral bills."

Again silence. Fargo knew that Stoneman did indeed have the gun pointed at his back. He also knew that Stoneman would not shoot. It would be easier for him to pay the extra five thousand.

He heard the shuddering rasp of breath behind him. Then Stoneman said, "All right, Fargo. Turn around and sit down. I'll meet your terms. There's nobody else I can hire with as much brass as you. Fifteen more now and twenty when you get back. But I expect results."

"You'll get 'em," Fargo said, eyes still on the thugs beyond the door.

"Then, leave us," Stoneman said to them. Like wraiths, they vanished.

"All right," Stoneman added. "Now, Fargo, let's talk business."

Fargo turned, as the shaking hand laid down its gun. "Suits me," he said . . .

Two weeks later, Stoneman's private yacht nosed into the Harbor of Belize, the capital of British Honduras, with Fargo aboard.

Take all the lousy little Central American towns that were ever built, Fargo thought, once he was ashore — roll them up into one, then spread them out again — then you had Belize.

The single British toehold on this end of the continent, it had been founded by stranded buccaneers centuries before. A malarial hellhole on the Caribbean coast, it contained maybe eight thousand people, some Indian, some Mestizo, damned few English. Beyond it stretched trackless wilderness, grazing land and jungle in which the rivers were the only roads. British Honduras backed up to Quintana Roo, a province of Mexico so wild, deserted, it did not even qualify as a state. It was flanked by Guatemala, where Fargo, thanks to certain activities on the losing side a year or two before, was wanted to the tune of two hundred dollars American — enough to make a Guatemalan rich for life.

That did not bother him. In khakis, with the cavalry hat jaunty on his head, he took a hack to the best hotel, which was not much. He wore his pistol openly on his hip, set for a cross-draw; the Batangas knife was sheathed on the other hip. His other weapons were in the trunk, stuck in the boot of the cab drawn by a thin, rickety animal.

His room was big, high ceilinged, hot as the hinges of hell, with a jalousied door and windows that looked out onto a paved court. Mosquito netting hung over the lumpy bed. He put the trunk on the bed, took out his weapons, checked them, oiled those that needed it, and shoved the trunk beneath the cot after having retrieved one of his three bottles of American bourbon. He pulled the cork with his teeth, took a long swallow, set the bottle on the battered chest that was the only other furnishing in the room, and then went downstairs.

There was a bar and dining room in which the air seemed not to have been changed since the founding of the colony. It was deserted, except for a sleepy Negro barman. Fargo asked what sort of whiskey they had and was surprised to find Scotch in long supply. He took a glass of the smoky stuff and sat down at a table, back, as usual, to the wall.

While he sipped his drink he contemplated what lay ahead of him.

The Valley of Skulls. Stoneman had pointed it out on the map. It was deep in the Lacándon rain forest, and the only safe access for Fargo to it was through British Honduras and Quintana Roo — so primitive that the word of revolution would not have reached it. He could not go through Guatemala because of the reward out for him, and he could not take the short route in because of the flare-up of bandits and revolutionaries in Yucatan, Campeche, and Chiapas itself.

The landing of Stoneman's yacht at any port there would have been a signal to draw the vultures, and they would have stayed with him all the way to his destination — if they did not kill him first for his guns and outfit.

So he would have to work his way in through British Honduras and Quintana Roo, through jungle broken only by the *monterías*, the hell-hole logging camps of Mexico, where enslaved Indians were driven until they fell to get out the fine mahogany of the region. Under the best of circumstances, it would have been a brutal trip to the Valley of Skulls; this way, it was going to be close to impossible. And yet, he had taken Stoneman's money and he was going to do it . . . somehow, some way.

Tossing off the glass of Scotch, signaling for the bottle to be brought, he remembered the rest of his session with the gaunt and withered old man. "All right, Stoneman. Exactly how many people have I got to bring out?"

"There are four Americans. Dr. Telford;

his daughter Nancy; Telford's assistant, a man named Norris; and my son Ned."

"Wait a minute," Fargo said. "There's a woman?"

"Nancy Telford's my son's fiancée, Fargo. Also, she's an excellent archeologist in her own right. She's used to roughing it."

"All the same, I didn't count on a woman."

Stoneman's eyes narrowed. "Your price is already set. Don't try to raise it again."

"No," Fargo had said. "No, I won't. But go on. How many other jokers are there in this deck?"

"I told you that there was something valuable, something rare, that I want brought out with them. It'll be a heavy load, Fargo. You'll need mules."

Fargo frowned. "It won't be easy getting mules into a place like that."

"Which is your problem. For forty thousand dollars, I'm sure you can solve it. According to the information I have, you'll need at least six pack animals."

His mouth was a thin, bloodless line. "I didn't pay a fortune to finance that expedition, Fargo, to have what it has uncovered left behind there in the jungle. They have unearthed certain items that, to me at least, are beyond price. I want those brought out. Even if . . . "

He hesitated. Fargo looked at him keenly. "Even if what?"

"Even if you have to leave some of the people behind," the old main said. "Not my son, of course. You're to bring him with you, no matter what. But . . . Well, he'll show you what you must bring out. And if you have to choose between the cargo and the people, the cargo comes first. Do you understand?"

"No," said Fargo. "What is this stuff that's so valuable?" He looked around, gestured. "Statues, masks, monuments? More of this stuff? You're loaded with it already. You'd doublecross your own expedition to get another load? Hell, that stuff's lain out in the jungle for centuries. It could stay there until things quiet down. You could wait; it won't rot."

"I *cannot* wait!" Stoneman's eyes glittered. "I'm old, Fargo, and my time's running out. All my life I've dreamed of seeing, touching, feeling, *possessing* the — what this expedition's uncovered. You'll see it soon enough and you'll understand then why. Meantime, what you don't know won't hurt you, I assure you. But take my word for it: what Telford and Ned have uncovered in the Valley of Skulls — what you are to bring to me — is worth anything and everything it cost: any amount of trouble, any amount of blood."

"And you still won't tell me what it is?"

"I said you'd learn in due time. When you reach the Valley of Skulls. I have reason for my secrecy, which you'll understand then. Meanwhile — forty thousand, Fargo. To bring me the cargo from the Valley of Skulls. No matter what you have to do."

Fargo hesitated. Then he grinned tightly. It stank; it stank to high heaven. But few jobs that paid off in that kind of cash didn't. All right, Stoneman was covering a hole card. But as long as he came across, what difference did it make?

"Okay, Stoneman," he said. "You're on. I'll take the job. For forty thousand, I'll guarantee you your son and the cargo, whatever it is, minimum. That price holds, even if the rest of 'em don't get out."

"Exactly. And . . . there's one more thing, Fargo."

"What's that?"

Stoneman's old, dry voice was cold and hard as iron.

"There may be moments in days to come when you're tempted to doublecross me. Before you do that, consider one thing."

"Which is − ?"

"That I'm one of the richest, most powerful men in the world. And that I know how to hate and hold a grudge, Fargo. And if you give me cause to, if you turn against me, I'll spend any amount of money, hire any number of men to find you wherever you are and teach you what it means to betray Ned Stoneman."

Fargo smiled faintly. "You're scaring me to death." Then his own eyes turned hard, despite the stretching of the smile to his wolf grin. "I'll do my job, Stoneman. But remember, that threat works both ways. You try to slip one to me, I'm a good hater, too. And you can't hire enough men to keep me from coming after you and getting you."

Stoneman looked back at him for a moment. Then he laughed, a short, harsh barking sound. "Yes, by God! We understand each other, don't we? You remind me of myself when I was young. All right, Fargo, we have a deal. Now, to details. I'll put my yacht at your disposal. It'll take you where you want to go and meet you wherever you plan to come out . . ."

Now, drinking more Scotch, Fargo considered. He could work his way through the jungle, make Chiapas somehow, buy the mules from one of the logging camps. After that, it would get trickier. Then he looked up, aware that the light had changed; someone was standing in the door. Suddenly, he tensed as he recognized that gigantic breadth of shoulder, the handsome face, the narrow hips, saw the thumbs of big hands hooked in the two criss-crossed *buscadero* belts that supported Colt .45's, Frontier Model. "Darnley!" he said.

"Well, damn my eyes," the other answered, his voice richly accented in the English way. "Neal Fargo. You bloody bastard, how the hell are you?" And he strode toward Fargo's table.

Fargo stood up. Darnley was as tall as he, two years younger, strikingly handsome in contrast to Fargo's scarred ugliness. He wore a khaki shirt, canvas pants, stockman's boots. His hand was big, hard. He was the second son of an English lord, a remittance man so wild, rough, and uncontrollable that his family had sent him to this colony to avoid a scandal at home and paid him a monthly wage to stay here. He was one of the best natural fighting men Fargo had ever met; and they had been in combat on the same side a couple of years before in Guatemala. There was a reward on Roger Darnley's head there, too. As they shook hands, Darnley asked, "Neal, what are you doing back in these parts?"

Fargo motioned him to a chair. "Drifting, Darnley. Just drifting."

The Englishman sat down, reached for the bottle, drank from its neck without waiting for a glass. "Not the way I hear it. You just got off a magnificent big white yacht."

Fargo's mouth twisted. "You really stay in touch, don't you?"

"That's my business."

"Oh, is it? And just what business are you in now?"

Darnley grinned, showing white, even teeth. His pale blue eyes danced with devil-may-care amusement. "About the same as you. A little of this, a little of that, the main thing the money and not too careful about the rest." Then he sobered.

"That was Stoneman's yacht — Ned D. Stoneman, the American oil man."

"Was it? I hadn't noticed."

Darnley laughed, but with less good humor this time. "Funny, you're not usually that careless. What is it, Fargo? What brings you back down here?"

"I said I was drifting."

"On Stoneman's yacht? Luxurious drifting."

"I go first class." Fargo took out a thin, black cigar, bit off its end, clamped it between his teeth. "Let's say I'm doing some oil prospecting for Stoneman."

"All right. We'll say that." Darnley signaled for a glass. "That doesn't mean I have to believe it."

"That's up to you," said Fargo.

"Oh, sure." The glass came; Darnley poured whiskey. Then he leaned forward. "What is it, Fargo? Something good? It must be something good to bring you down here." His eyes were pale and cold now. "And I want in."

"No," said Fargo. "It's nothing big and there's only room for one."

"You're wrong. There's got to be room for me. Otherwise, you don't operate."

Fargo took the cigar from his mouth. "What the hell you mean by that?"

"Oh, I've been busy since you last saw me, Fargo." The Englishman's smile came back easy, charming, but it did not deceive Fargo. He had seen Darnley smile just like that as he pulled the trigger to execute a wounded prisoner. "Or haven't you heard of Darnley's Raiders?"

"No."

"Well, you will. It's my own little army, Fargo. Well, not so little, either. Forty, fifty men. And all top-hole fighters, thoroughly experienced and tough as bootleather. You'd be surprised how many good men like that there are down here, Neal; this is a fine place to hide out. Your American Wild West is taming down, and the gunmen are pulling out. There are French outlaws stranded in Panama when the French gave up on their canal . . . Spanish *hidalgos* dispossessed by revolutions here and there;

English remittance men like myself; plus a few whites who've been here all their lives, grandsons and great grandsons of the old pirates and buccaneers. Darnley's Raiders, Fargo, and it's as tight and tough a little outfit as you're ever likely to see — and I run it!" He took out a cigarette. "We operate in British Honduras, on the Yucatan Peninsula or in Guatemala."

"You're wanted in Guatemala."

"I'm wanted in a lot of places. So are my men. We don't let that stop us." He snapped a match, lit his smoke. "We go where we please, when we please and nobody stands against us." His eyes met Fargo's. "Not you, not anyone."

"We'll see," Fargo said.

Darnley leaned back, negligently crossed his legs. "Oh, yes, I'm sure we will." He was abruptly serious again. "Look here, Fargo, I know you. You didn't come here for a rest cure; you came for money. You're always where the money is, like a vulture at the meat. Well, I'll tell you now; you deal us in."

"No," Fargo said.

"You're being stubborn."

"There's not enough to go around."

"There is if you're here for the reason I think you are."

Fargo rolled the cigar across his mouth. "Which is — ?"

"Stoneman's yacht. An expedition financed by Stoneman in the place called the Valley of Skulls, in Chiapas. They've found what they were looking for, and you're here to bring it out."

"Suppose I was. Some stone statues, that sort of thing. No money in those. Just Mayan relics."

Darnley looked at him strangely. Then a curious smile crossed that handsome face. "Fargo," he said, "you're slipping."

Something in his voice froze Fargo. He looked at Darnley carefully. "Am I?"

"You sure as hell are if you believe that stone statue business. Damn it, Fargo, you know you're here because they've found the Golden Gun!"

Neal Fargo neither moved a muscle

nor flickered an eye. But suddenly he understood. The memory of a legend, of stories told around a hundred campfires, came back suddenly. All at once it fitted; everything fell into place. Yes, he thought with rising excitement. Yes, that was it. Surely. That was why Stoneman was willing to shell out forty thousand; that was why the cargo he was to bring from the Valley of Skulls took precedence even over the lives of the members of the expedition. It all made sense now. Good sense. From Stoneman's viewpoint, anyhow.

"Nothing happens in my territory that I don't know about," continued Darnley, bending close, his voice a whisper. "Yucatan, Campeche, Quintana Roo, Chiapas, Guatemala, here . . . I have my spies, Fargo, everywhere. I knew that Stoneman had sent an expedition to the Lacándon Forest; I knew they were supposed to be digging for Mayan ruins. And then, a few days ago, I found out something else — something that ties in nicely with your presence here."

"Go on," said Fargo.

"They hired some Indians to help them dig. Somebody in that expedition — I hear it was Stoneman's son — played rough with them. Apparently he worked some of them to death and shot some others when they protested. Anyhow, one ran away, fled into the jungle. He made it to a *montería* in Campeche, a logging camp where I had a spy. Somewhere in the rain forest, he'd tangled with a jaguar and got himself torn up pretty badly; he lived just long enough to give a hint. Something they'd uncovered there, an old gun, he said, that made young Stoneman go almost crazy, threaten to kill them all if they touched it. I thought then, when I got the word, that it might be . . . now you show up on Stoneman's yacht. Two and two make four, Fargo. You're here to bring out the Golden Gun for Stoneman. Two thousand pounds of pure unalloyed Spanish gold. That's a lot of gold, Fargo, close to three-quarters of a million American dollars worth." He leaned back.

"Don't tell me," he finished, "there's not enough to go around."

Fargo said nothing, only poured another drink. His brain raced.

The Golden Gun. It was a legend in lower Mexico and the Caribbean. Spanish *conquistadores*, it was said, had prepared a special gift for the King of Spain. Ten cannons they had cast, not of steel or bronze, but of pure gold from the mines of Mexico and sent them home in a galleon guarded by a company of soldiers. But not even the awesome power of Spain could stand against the hurricanes that racked the Gulf of Mexico. The galleon had been caught in one, slammed ashore and broken up. All but one of its golden guns had gone to the bottom of the sea. One single, precious cannon had been salvaged by the survivors. But the Indians of the coast had attacked them and driven them inland. Southward, under constant attack by vengeful tribes, they had fought their way through the jungle, through what was now Campeche, into Chiapas. They hauled with them the golden cannon, their only artillery, the only thing that kept them alive, as they turned the field piece on the warriors who came after them. Finally, driven into refuge in the Lacándon Forest, caught between tribes from north and south alike, they had halted, forted up, made a last stand. But their gunpowder ran out; they were overwhelmed and slaughtered. Before they died, when they had fired their last charge from the golden cannon, they had buried it. Then they were massacred.

And yet the legend had lived after them — that somewhere, in the vast depths of that great rain forest, lay hidden a huge cannon of purest gold worth a king's ransom. And that, Fargo realized now, was the secret the archeologist must have discovered in the Library of Madrid; perhaps one survivor had made it back to Spanish civilization and lived long enough to tell his story. That was the inducement the scientist had used to persuade Stoneman to finance the expedition: that was what the six mules were to bring out of the Valley of Skulls, the cargo more precious than any life save that of Stoneman's son.

Fargo took a drink. He had, in a sense, been taken. He saw that now. What he had figured on having to bring out was more of the statues, slabs, other relics of the sort with which Stoneman's town house was crammed. Such things were so common down here that no one really gave a damn for them — not the Mexican bandits and revolutionaries, not the Indians, not soldiers of fortune like Darnley. Still, it was tough enough to haul even those out of that terrible jungle; forty thousand was a fair price for such a job. But three-quarters of a million in gold? Good God, thought Fargo, if Darnley were right, that golden gun would bring down on him every buzzard, every gun-toter and robber and soldier of fortune in this end of the world!

His mouth twisted. He'd let himself be taken, all right; this was a job worth twice what he'd agreed to. And yet he'd given his word, and the value of his word was as important as his skill with guns when it came to making a living the hard way he had chosen. But, damn! The prospect of the Golden Gun had already drawn Darnley to him, Darnley and his army. And now he would have to fight them all to get the gun to Stoneman.

His face never changed; he reached for the bottle again. He knew Darnley; not even he would stand a chance against the Englishman backed up with the kind of soldiers the remittance man had gathered. He couldn't fight Darnley; and so there was only one other thing to do: he would have to use him . . .

There was a way he could do that: let Darnley and his men help him bring out the gun. Then it would be up to him to get it away from them when they had come back to civilization.

And so, without the flicker of an eye, he made his decision. "You know," he said, "there might be something in what you say. Maybe there's enough to go around after all. Why don't we talk some business?"

"Now, that's better." Darnley grinned. He shoved back his chair. "But not here. I'll have a *mozo* rustle up a horse for you. Then we'll have one more drink and ride."

4

"THIS is the way I see it," Darnley said, as they loped along a sandy road between alternate stretches of jungle and swampy grassland. "Nobody could reach this Valley of Skulls through Mexico now; that's a damned bucket of rattle-snakes. You'd have to go in through the narrow part of Guatemala. Bring the people and the gun out the same way, by the back door, so to speak. Well, I've got connections all along the line. If we work together, I can make it a lot easier, Fargo. Then, when we get the cannon out, we can cut it up, melt it down — "

"No," said Fargo.

"No?" Darnley twisted in the saddle, looked at him.

"You melt it down, it's three-quarters of a million in gold. Leave it like it is, bring it out intact, it's a million, maybe more."

"Damned if I figure that."

Fargo grinned tautly. "You don't know Stoneman. Money he's got. He loves it like his life's-blood, true. But, more than that, he wants something nobody else has got — he wants the only golden Spanish cannon left in the world; it's his lifelong dream. He makes a million every week, maybe sooner; I don't think he'll balk at putting up a week's pay for a gun like that."

"You mean he wants the cannon as a museum piece, not for the gold in it?"

"He's a collector, a pack rat. He wants that cannon whole, complete, and he'll pay any price to get it."

"So, if we bring it out, we hang on to it, hold it for ransom, he pays the ransom."

"That's the size of it," Fargo said. They reined in, let the horses drink from a rivulet that trickled across the road. In the jungle that made walls on either side, monkeys and strange birds screeched; it was near dusk and the animals were more active.

"And even though he's paid you down, you're willing to go against him."

"I hired out to bring out the members of the expedition and cargo for six mules. I didn't count on that cargo being something that would bring down every man with a gun in this end of the world on me. I'll deliver the expedition to Belize, to his yacht. I'll deliver six mules of statues and such like, too. The gun comes extra — mighty extra."

Darnley laughed. "That sounds like the old Fargo I used to know."

Fargo gathered rein, touched the horse with his heels. They rode on. "If you knew about the gun, why did you declare me in? Why didn't you just go after it yourself?"

"Because that would put me up against you. I'd rather have you with me than against me, Neal. I know you too well. I might have an army, but if I had to fight you, that might not help me too much. This way, partners, we're both sure of success . . . and profit." He gestured. "The ranch is right around the bend."

They made the turn. The jungle gave way to a wide, grassy clearing studded with palms. In its center was a sprawl of log buildings, corrals with horses. "I bought this place quite legally," Darnley said, "with the scores I made outside the colony. I don't want His Majesty's government on me if I can help it, and I mind my manners reasonably well here in British Honduras. In fact, my men occasionally serve as special police when there's trouble in the back country. We don't really ranch here; it's just our barracks, so to speak."

"Nice layout," Fargo said, as they rode into the yard.

"Yes." said Darnley. "Incidentally, I'm the only one who knows about the Golden Gun. Until our plans are firm, let's not mention it among the others."

Fargo grinned crookedly. "Leaves you leeway for a double cross if you need it."

"I play honestly with my men. But they're pretty hard customers. Some of them might not return the compliment.

77

I don't want them to get any ideas of double-crossing me and going into business for themselves." He touched one of the Colts on his hip. "I'm faster and harder than any of them, so far. That's how I stay on top." He pulled up before the largest structure of the place. "This is my headquarters. You'll stay here with me."

They swung down and a *mozo*, half Indian, half black, came to take the horses. The building before them was big, solid, built of fine mahogany. Darnley pushed open the door and they went in.

The room was long, dim; there were several trestle tables, and men sat around them playing cards, drinking. One or two of them had Indian girls on their laps and pawed them. Everybody stopped what he was doing and looked up as the two men entered.

"Gentlemen," Darnley said, standing there with widespread legs, thumbs hooked in gunbelts. "Gentlemen, a new member of our mess. Some of you

78

may have heard of Neal Fargo, from America."

Fargo's eyes swept the lamplit room alertly. Darnley had been right; they were hard customers, all right: men with the stamp of outlawry on them, guns and knives draped all over them. Then he stiffened as a blocky, familiar figure shoved an Indian girl off its lap and stood up.

"Neal Fargo," the man said. He was short, thick, muscular, and his beard was iron gray. He wore a Panama hat, a blue workshirt, canvas pants. His eyes were like gray, steel marbles beneath thick brows, his nose craggy and often broken. On his right hip hung a Bisley colt in a half-breed bolster; on his left was a huge, old-fashioned Bowie knife in a fringed sheath. "By God."

Fargo stood loosely. "Hello, Brassfield. Long time no see."

The man's voice was deep, harsh. "You're goddamn right long time no see. Not since you killed my brother in Cheyenne."

"He shouldn't have come after me with that knife," said Fargo. "He didn't know how to use it."

Suddenly the room was silent. A kind of corridor formed on either side, so that Brassfield and Fargo were looking straight up and down it at one another. Even Darnley stepped aside a pace or two. "I didn't know you knew each other."

"Yes," said Fargo. "The Brassfields were pretty good train robbers in their time. But they outlived their time."

"You were bounty hunting," Brassfield rasped.

"I needed cash. The reward on you two was fat. Nothing personal, Brassfield. If your brother had come along peaceable."

"Peaceable," Brassfield said thinly. "And the rest of his life in prison."

"A man does what he has to when he needs to earn a buck. You robbed trains. I collected scalps. The reward for your brother was payable dead or alive. I would have taken him in alive if he'd let me."

Brassfield's thick chest rose and fell with sucked-in, let-out breath. "No matter," he said. "Vic's dead now. And you will be in a few minutes."

"Now, wait a minute, Brassfield — " Darnley's voice crackled.

"No," Fargo said. "If he's got something to settle with me, let's get it over with. Brassfield. You mean it?"

"I mean it, Fargo."

"Guns or knives?"

Brassfield's mouth warped beneath the beard. "You took my brother with a knife. But he didn't know cold steel the way I do, Fargo. Nobody knows cold steel the way I do."

"Then knives," said Fargo.

"Yeah. Knives."

"Outdoors? In here?"

"It's too dark outdoors," said Brassfield. "God, Fargo, you don't know how long I've been waiting for this chance."

"Well make the most of it," Fargo said. "The rest of you stand back and give us room."

There was a general exodus to the

walls. Then Fargo and Brassfield were alone in the center of the room, between the tables, both of them standing easily. It had been a long time, Fargo thought. The Brassfields had kept on robbing trains well after everybody else had given it up; Al Jennings was in jail, Cassidy and his Wild Bunch had fogged out and disappeared, but the Brassfields stayed with it. And so the reward had been too tempting to turn down. But it had been a fair fight, except that Lon Brassfield was right; his brother Vic had been good with cold steel, but not a genius. Fargo was a genius. On the other hand, from what he had heard, Lon Brassfield was, too.

It was, he thought with a kind of savage pleasure, going to be a damned good fight.

"Come ahead, Lon," he said and drew the Batangas knife, and his wrist flicked and the handles dropped into place, unfolded, within his palm, and ten inches of narrow, razor-edged steel glittered in the lamplight.

"Yeah," Brassfield said, and he drew the Bowie and went into a knife-fighter's crouch, hunched, gut protected, side presented.

They moved cautiously toward one another in the total silence of the huge room. The Bowie had a twelve-inch blade, and it was as good for hacking as for thrusting. Fargo's lighter knife lacked the weight for that sort of combat, but that did not bother him. His stance matched Brassfield's as they edged closer, lightly balanced on the balls of their feet.

Two yards away, Brassfield stopped. "By the way, Fargo. Don't try to shift hands and guard on me. I know you can use your left hand good as your right. You won't take me by surprise that way."

"Thanks for telling me," Fargo said. "Otherwise, I might have left you an openin'."

"I'll find one," said Brassfield. He came in fast then, swiftly as a striking snake.

Fargo saw the big Bowie blade wink

out. He slacked his right leg, sagged, opened his left arm, and the steel went between bicep and torso, missing flesh. Then he pivoted, wheeled away, clear, and came in from the flank; but where his blade should have taken unprotected flesh, it met hard steel. Brassfield was every bit as quick and canny with a knife as he, had recovered, parried, and finely tempered steel chimed, bell-like, as their blades met.

With a shock that Fargo felt all the way up his arm. Brassfield had muscle, too. He turned the Bowie, tried to use its leverage to wrench Fargo's knife away, but Fargo let the Batangas blade slide off without resisting and slashed in again and was met by Brassfield again, and this time Brassfield's knife edged past Fargo's guard and drew blood along the inside of his arm.

That was too close, thought Fargo, backing swiftly. A half inch more and the tendons would have gone, the artery spouted blood. This was a fight that would take every ounce of speed, skill, strength and ingenuity.

The hush was total as they circled, maneuvered. Fargo thought of the two fighting cocks in the ring in San Antonio. The same, exactly the same. Brassfield charged; Fargo sidestepped, Brassfield had expected it, turned, Fargo parried just in time. The Batangas knife slid down the Bowie blade, locked it for a moment, and they were face to face.

Brassfield's breath was foul. "Next time," he rasped, eyes glittering, confident. He broke the lock, and Fargo dodged back just in time to keep from being gutted. Off balance, he had to yield and yield again as Brassfield came in hard, the long, heavy, sharp blade flickering and slashing, dangerous on stroke or backstroke, either one.

Brassfield came in harder and harder on the offensive, giving Fargo no chance to stand and fight, regain balance. "Hah!" Brassfield made that sound with every swordlike stroke and dagger thrust. "Hah, hah, hah!" And their blades rang and chimed and belled.

Then something struck Fargo behind the knees.

A bench, slewed crosswise from one of the tables. He saw the gleam of triumph in Brassfield's eyes; this was what he had been driving for. Slam Fargo up against the bench, off balance, then lunge and get him. All that went through Fargo's head in a split second, even as he parried again; then he moved back a little more, tripped over the bench and fell sprawling on his back as he evaded Brassfield's thrust.

He landed hard, open and vulnerable, and Brassfield's mouth twisted, his yellow teeth shining in the depths of his beard. Brassfield leaped the bench and came in for the kill, thrusting downward, and now Fargo had his opening. Too eager, too sure, Brassfield almost fell on him and Fargo rolled and thrust upward with the Batangas knife and felt it enter flesh, deep and hard. He turned it and ripped just as Brassfield's Bowie plunged into the hardpacked dirt floor where Fargo had just been. And then Fargo was on his knees, lifting Brassfield impaled on his knife, as Brassfield's body went dead and the Bowie dropped from his hand. Fargo had fallen backward over the bench deliberately, landing exactly right, gathered, ready, tempting Brassfield, and his opponent had taken the bait. When Brassfield had leaped the bench and come down, he had been the one off balance, the one vulnerable, and that had killed him. Now, gutted from groin to breastbone, Brassfield swayed backward, fell off of Fargo's blade, landed on his back, kicked once, made a strange sound, and then was still.

Withdrawing the Batangas knife, which was reddened to the hilt, Fargo stood there, panting.

"Christ, man," said Darnley. "You ripped him wide-open."

Fargo clenched his teeth against an upsurge of bile. Though he was trembling with reaction, coolly he knelt and wiped the blade clean against Brassfield's thigh. Then he folded the handles and returned the knife to its sheath.

"Yes," he said. He looked around, hand on his Colt. "Brassfield got any friends resent that?"

Nobody spoke or moved. Except the girl who had been on Brassfield's lap. She was Indian, very young, not over seventeen. Her eyes wide, her small-nosed, pretty face blank with surprise, breasts the size of melons, she looked from the body on the floor to Fargo. Then she said, in Spanish, "*Señor. Gracias. Nombre de Dios, gracias!*"

It was not what Fargo had expected. "You were his girl?" he asked in Spanish.

"His slave. He was a dog, a beast. Thank God you've freed me from him. I hated him." Then she spat violently on the weltering body.

"All right, Fargo." Darnley laughed shortly. "Her name's Luz. I guess she's yours; spoils of war." Then he barked: "Clean up this mess, you people hear? Drag him out, wipe up the blood! I'll not have this mess in my headquarters."

Somebody asked numbly: "Bury him? Tonight?"

"Bury him, hell!" Darnley snapped. "Drag him to the forest. Let the jaguars and the vultures and the ants bury him. Just take him far enough so he won't stink." Then he turned to Fargo. "Neal, you must be hungry. What about some dinner?"

The thought of food made Fargo's stomach clench.

"A drink first," he said.

"Right," said Darnley. "You've earned it. A fresh bottle." He snapped orders to another woman. She shuffled off, came back with an uncorked bottle of Scotch and passed it to Fargo. He drank, long and deeply. When he lowered the bottle he said, "Now, I can eat."

Darnley's bedroom was small, off the main room. There was a cot with a mosquito bar, a table, a couple of chairs, and books piled all around; Darnley was a great reader. Centipedes and ants crawled, however, in and out between the pages. In this climate, the creatures bred everywhere.

Darnley poured more Scotch and passed it over. "You see, Neal you'd never have made it on your own, anyhow. Oh, you'd probably have gotten there, sneaking through the jungle . . . nobody's better in the jungle than you, I know that. But with a bunch of scientists and six mule loads? You'd never have gotten out again. Not when the word went around that those six mules were hauling a ton of gold."

He smiled, drank. "This way, you have an escort. Everybody knows Darnley's Raiders and is scared to death of 'em. We can take the short way through Guatemala in and out, both. Their army won't dare tackle my whole outfit. Now, the way I see it is this: I send messengers ahead. We go up the rivers by boat, cross from one river to another, everything will be ready, waiting. I have friends in all the *monterías*, the logging camps. Well, not friends, really; they pay for protection from Darnley's Raiders, but they'll do what I say. We won't have any trouble getting to the Valley of the Skulls — if you know where it is."

"I know where it is," said Fargo.

"You have a map, of course."

Fargo grinned. "You know me better than that, Darnley."

"You mean it's in your head."

"That's right."

"The same old Fargo; never take a chance."

"Not an unnecessary one. I can memorize a map. As long as it's locked up in my brain there's no profit in anybody killing me to take it off my carcass."

Darnley looked hurt.

"You don't trust me?"

Fargo grinned back. "Darnley, I don't know how many people are in this world. Out of all those millions or billions, though, there's exactly one — no more — that I trust. He was my commander in the Rough Riders and he used to be President of the United States. I'd put my life in his hands; I wouldn't give anybody else the time of day."

"Nor I," said Darnley. He smiled. "But as long as we're watching each other . . . very well, Fargo. You call the shots and lead the way. We'll tag along." He yawned. "It's been a long day, Neal. You can take Brassfield's room. He was my Number Two until you fought him. It's right next door. Bunk in; tomorrow we'll move your gear from the hotel."

"Sure," Fargo said. He arose. "Good night, Darnley."

It was not, he thought, as he went out, the way he had counted on working this job. But nothing ever worked out the way you figured, anyhow, and a smart man made use of whatever came to hand. So he would use Darnley and his raiders, let them help him to get to the Valley of Skulls and get the gun out. What he had told Darnley about holding it for ransom would stifle any impulse Darnley might have to cut the gun up at once and divide the gold. How he would get it away intact from Darnley later on was a bridge he'd cross when he came to it. For now, he had to keep the Englishman's confidence.

He pushed through the door next to Darnley's room. When he entered, he was surprised to find a lamp burning. There was a table, chairs, a mosquito-netted cot. Fargo stared at what lay behind the netting.

The girl Luz, stretched her naked body invitingly, looking at him through the gauze.

"*Señor*," she whispered.

The spoils of war, thought Fargo, and his wolfish grin tugged his face. He was tired, all right, but not too tired for that.

"Hello, Luz," he said, and began to strip off his clothes.

5

TWO weeks later, Fargo, the double-barreled Fox shotgun slung over his shoulder, his Winchester cradled on his lap, rode the prow of a dugout canoe up a nameless river through the jungle.

Behind him, Darnley, with a Lee-Enfield rifle and his two holstered sixguns, lounged, smoking. And behind Darnley, seven Indians paddled.

It took all seven of them to propel the craft, rudely made and heavily loaded with supplies, up the swift stream. Their brown bodies glistened in the dim light of the silent rain forest as their arms moved in unison.

Strung out behind them were twenty more canoes, each containing two of Darnley's Raiders armed to the teeth. Also making the trip were the necessary Indians, who were being paid well, not in money, but in cloth and rum.

They had switched rivers three times, trekking through the jungle in between. At each new stream, true to Darnley's word, canoes had been waiting. That, Fargo thought, had made things much easier.

Even so, they were hard enough, He had brought mosquito repellent, but these insects seemed to live off it, drink it like nectar. So, too, did the biting, stinging gnats. Then there were the leeches and the great ticks and the bugs that burrowed under your toenails and laid their eggs there. The insect life alone would have been enough to drive an ordinary man mad; then, add to that the stifling tropic heat, the ever-present danger of venomous snakes, the countless grueling portages around rapids and falls; and top it all off with the threat of the jungle Indians.

The jungle tribes were all around them, their presence felt. They were close to the border now between Guatemala and Mexico, and this was the haunt of the various tribes grouped all together under the designation Lacándon. Fargo had seen them before: they were a handsome people, the men of a beauty almost as great as that of their women, and they were wholly wild. They still used poisoned arrows and darts fired from blowguns, as well as a few old blunderbusses garnered from what few civilized expeditions dared to penetrate this area. They were out there now in the jungle, following, waiting. But they would not attack; not against forty heavily armed men. It would have been different, though, Fargo thought, if he had been trying to make this journey alone.

Darnley gave an order. The lead canoe put in to a great sandbar on the river's edge. "We'll camp here for the night," the Englishman said, getting out.

"It's early," Fargo said.

"We need meat. I'm going to send out hunting parties." As the men clambered ashore, Darnley ranked them up like soldiers. Looking at them, Fargo pondered again the fact that he had never seen such a hardcase group gathered under a single banner. Every one of them was an expert fighting man, seasoned and utterly ruthless.

Darnley sent half of them to the jungle. Carrying rifles, pistols, shotguns, they moved off into the pathless jungle in various directions. The rest ranged themselves in a perimeter guard around the camp. The big, young Englishman stalked back to Fargo, cigarette waggling between his teeth. "What about you? Shall we do our share of hunting?"

"Why not?" Fargo had no stomach for lounging idly around camp.

"*Bueno.*" Darnley turned, barked orders. Two Indians came up the river bank carrying short spears with steel heads. Darnley grinned, took the spears, then turned to Fargo holding one out.

Fargo looked at it, grinned. "Have you ever done that?"

"No, I'm eager to try it. They say it's great sport."

"It is if you're lucky."

Darnley frowned. "What do you mean by lucky?"

"If you're lucky, you don't meet a jaguar at all. If you're just a little bit lucky, you run into one but he doesn't charge you. If you're unlucky, he charges; and if you're very unlucky, you don't hold that spear just right when he jumps. And they bury you. If they think that much of you."

"You've really done it? You've killed a jaguar with a spear?"

"Twice," said Fargo. He plucked at the heavy bandoliers criss-crossed over his chest; his shirt was sodden beneath them. Then he threw the spear Darnley had given him back to its owner. "You can try yours if you want to. I don't have anything to prove. I'll stick to the Fox sawed-off if one comes at me quick."

"All right," said Darnley. "You can cover me."

"You go to hell," said Fargo. "If you're nuts enough to take on *el Tigre* with a spear, that's between you and him. You can take the consequences."

"You mean you wouldn't shoot if I were being mauled by a cat?"

Fargo looked at Darnley and rolled his cigar across his mouth.

"You're a little bit younger than I am. One thing you still got to learn. Don't run around playing hero unless you aim to play hero all the way. Why should you go into it knowin' I'm gonna bail you out if things go wrong? Why are you entitled to an advantage over the cat?"

Darnley frowned. "You're a hell of a bloke. You'd let a jaguar kill me if I miss him with the spear?"

Fargo grinned around the cigar. "Like I said, if you want to meet him hand to hand, that's between you and him."

"Fargo, I don't understand you at all."

"Damn few people do," Fargo said. "Not even me, always. You want to kill some meat, I'll help you. But you want to play games, that's your lookout. I didn't come into this jungle to play games." He threw the cigar butt away. "Let's go huntin'," he said.

He had been offhanded about it because there was not really much chance that they would meet a jaguar. The big cats were deadly, far worse than American mountain lions, but they were shy and clever. Even with the Indian tracker running ahead, Fargo doubted that they would get more than a few monkeys; likely they would dine on fish caught by the canoemen.

Then, where a rivulet crossed the sodden floor of the forest, the Indian tracker grunted, pointed. And Fargo and Darnley saw them; the fresh pug marks, so new they were not quite full yet with oozing water.

"Well," said Darnley. He grinned and hefted the spear. "We might have some luck after all."

"Maybe," Fargo said. He knelt, inspected the tracks. Then his backbone turned cool; a kind of shiver walked down his spine. "You'll have some luck if we cross this stream and go into that scrub yonder."

Darnley blinked. "What do you mean?"

"One of these prints is outsize, swollen, puffy as hell. That jaguar's taken a wound, maybe in a fight over a female, maybe a snakebite. But he's got a bad foot full of pus. He left some of the pus in this print. That's a wounded animal in there, Darnley."

"You think he'll bay, then; charge?"

"Good chance." Fargo unslung the shotgun. "And the light ain't good. You'd better lay aside the spear and figure on usin' one of those Colts or let it ride until tomorrow."

"No," said Darnley.

"Don't be a fool," Fargo said.

Darnley stroked his cleft chin. "I'm not. Fargo, you've always been the toughest man I've ever known. That's bothered me."

Fargo looked at him. "Darnley," he said.

"Yeah."

"You know what you're saying?"

"I'm saying I want that jaguar. With this spear."

"No," said Fargo. "You don't want

that jaguar, you want me."

"I don't understand."

"You're beginning to catch the fever. Hell, I've dodged it all over the West and Mexico. A man gets a reputation with a gun, everybody that thinks he's tough has to try him out. What you're saying is you're matching yourself against me with that jaguar. After the jaguar, what? Will you try to come up against me with those?" He pointed to Darnley's holstered Colts.

Darnley stared at him, then laughed shortly. "Fargo, we're partners, not enemies."

Fargo sucked in a breath, let it out. "Yeah," he said. "Let's hope it stays that way. Okay, Darnley, go after your jaguar. But you're on your own; don't expect me to bail you out."

Darnley's mouth thinned. "Very well," he said and crossed the stream.

Fargo watched how, in the damp green twilight of the jungle, Darnley moved across the clearing beneath huge trees toward the wall of bamboo scrub. Big, muscular, young and full of strength, he went in a crouch, the short spear thrust out before him. Fargo chewed a wooden match. Yeah, he thought. This jaguar; then another. And then we're even. After that . . . the guns?

But for now he stood with the shotgun in his hand and watched the Englishman stalk forward toward the wall of brush. Somewhere beyond that green bastion, a wounded jaguar, a big tom by the looks, was holed up; it had taken flight just ahead of them. Now, nursing its festering paw, it was likely to be proddy; let Darnley even shake that bamboo and . . .

The damned fool was going straight into the thicket. The bamboo rattled, clashed, as Darnley thrust his way between the canes.

"Jesus Christ," Fargo said and leaped the stream, raising the shotgun.

Then came the short, harsh cough. The bamboo rattled. Darnley tumbled back into the clearing. He tripped, landed flat on his shoulders, spear pointed up. Hard after him came a blur of tawny spotted killer, a hundred and fifty pounds of hurting, enraged cat. Snarling horribly, it threw itself at Darnley, claws gleaming in the dying light, unsheathed.

Darnley thrust upward with the spear, then rolled.

The squall that filled the jungle was a hideous sound. The steel-headed spear caught the cat behind its rib-cage, reached up through its guts. It lashed out with all four feet; one hind paw caught Darnley's thigh as he got to his knees, ripped his pants, sent blood coursing. Then Darnley was over the cat, had it pinned on is back, bore down on the spear, grinning like a madman. The huge animal clawed and flailed helplessly, twisting and turning on the point. Then its blood welled out; it kicked, lay still. Panting, Darnley kept grinding the spearhead in. Beside him, the Indian stood frozen, wide-eyed, hand over mouth.

Darnley put a booted foot on the cat's belly, pulled loose the spear. He held it erect, letting the blood trickle down its shaft over his hand. In the dim light his blue eyes gleamed. "Fargo. You see?"

"Yes," Fargo said. "Yes, I see, Darnley." He felt tired and sad, for now he was afraid he would have to kill the Englishman before this deal was finished, and that was something he did not want to do. But Darnley had it; like the fighting cock in the San Antonio ring, he had it: the need always to pit himself against someone as good.

Just let him hold off, Fargo thought, until we get that golden gun out. "Let the Indian drag the carcass," he said, "and let's go back to camp."

Long before they crossed the border into Mexico, Fargo knew they had nothing to fear from the Guatemalan army. It was supposed to be guarding the frontier, but Darnley had sent word ahead that he was coming and the soldiers had prudently got the hell out of his way. They would never have known they were in another country if it had not been for Fargo's instruments.

He had traveled in rain forest like this before. A compass was all right, it helped. But there were times when you had to have closer, definite bearings; this was as lonesome and unland-marked a place as the open sea and could only be traversed by the same sort of navigation. So he had a compass and a sextant and an astrolabe and a set of climber's spikes like those used by the timber toppers of the Douglas fir logging camps. He also had a safety rope. Every night he scaled one of the forest giants and took a reading on stars invisible from below. Then he plotted, checked it against the data in his head, and made whatever adjustments were necessary to get them to the Valley of Skulls.

A day after they'd passed the frontier, they reached a *montería*. Here a dock thrust out into the broadening river, and heavy chains impounded enormous, restless logs. They put in, climbed out. And the first thing Fargo saw was the ant-and-vulture-picked body of a man hanging by its neck from a tree near the river.

There was not much left of the man; white bone showed through seething corruption. Fargo turned his head away and spat. Then there was a shout from the dock. "*Señor* Darnley!"

Beside Fargo, Darnley muttered: "Don Pepe Tarano, the *contratista* of this camp."

Fargo looked at the stocky man with the drinker's belly through narrowed eyes as, followed by a crew of plug-uglies, slit-mouthed Indians bearing Winchesters, Tarano waddled up to Darnley, seized his hand. "Welcome, Don Roger. A rare honor, what brings you here? My poor house is yours . . ."

While that was going on, Fargo swept his gaze around the lumber camp. A big clearing chopped out of the jungle, hovels for barracks, better quarters for mules more valuable than the men who handled them. The timber rights to these huge forests were owned by grandees in Mexico City, big politicos. They leased them out in turn to *contratistas*, the contractors who recruited the illiterate, dirt-poor Indians of Southern Mexico into bondage by promising them twenty, thirty dollars a year hard cash wages. Say this of course for the *contratista*, Fargo thought; as often as not, the men they hired were outlaws and killers fleeing from the law; not only innocent *peones*. That was why their *capos*, their gang bosses, carried pistols and huge whips. In a *montería*, a man worked until he died. Things were rigged so he could never pay his debt of advanced money; and, just before he died, he usually rebelled. Probably the corpse hanging from the tree by the river was that of such a desperate man. It was slavery, pure and simple — one of the reasons Mexico was continually racked by revolution. But for the moment, that was no concern of Fargo's. What they needed now was mules, and Darnley had said they could get them here.

They walked through the clearing toward the headquarters building, Darnley's

Raiders strung out behind them with guns significantly at the ready. They were indeed as tough a bunch as Fargo had ever seen, especially the English and the tropic-hardened Frenchmen from Panama. Even the tough gunmen of the *montería* shrank back in the face of that army.

In Don Pepe's dirt-floored casa, where an ugly, full-breasted, pot-bellied *Tzeltál* concubine served them *pulque*, Fargo leaned back in his chair while the fat *contratista* and Darnley argued over mules. Here their worth was double that of horses, which soon sickened and died in the miserable climate. Fargo listened boredly, sipping *pulque* until he heard Darnley's voice rise. "I want two dozen mules. You sell them to me at that price, or else I take them."

"But you are robbing me, Señor Darnley!"

Darnley's eyes were like two chips of ice. "I can rob you worse."

Pepe swelled like a puffing toad, then collapsed. "Sí. I cannot fight Darnley's

Raiders. You shall have your mules."

They spent the night there. Just before dusk, the daily whippings took place — Indians who had failed to fill their quota of work or had otherwise transgressed. One man died under the lash; unremitting labor and inadequate food left him no strength to endure a beating. His corpse was rolled into the river and the current roiled it southward. The rest, even the beaten men, went to eat their scanty supper and take what pleasure they could arrange with the Mestizo washerwomen-whores.

That night, Fargo climbed a tree, to the awe of the lumbermen below. He took his bearings on the stars, determined their course for tomorrow.

After they left the *montería*, they pushed into jungle that had never been penetrated by man; not, at least, by white men in this century. Their *macheteros* worked like machines ahead of them, clearing a path, blades flashing rhythmically. Fargo, Darnley, the army and the mules came on behind.

He shot the sun; he shot the stars; he guided them according to the memorized back-azimuths in his head. Somehow he brought them through that jungle, across three hundred miles of wilderness, exactly to the place for which he aimed. A week beyond the *montería*, deep in Chiapas now, they heard gunfire before they saw the Valley of Skulls.

On a jungled ridge crest Fargo tensed. "Darnley."

"I hear it," the Englishman said.

"How far off, you judge?"

"Two miles, maybe three."

Fargo cocked his head. "Way I make it, there's three, four guns against two dozen."

"About that," Darnley said.

"Two, three miles through this country will take the rest of the day." Fargo turned. "Let me have that machete." He took the broad-bladed knife from an Indian.

Darnley's eyes kindled. "What — ?"

Fargo gestured. "The Valley of Skulls.

It's down there. Some damned *revolucionarios* or bandits have found that place. Those few guns can't stand off all the rest. I'm going down there, around, flank 'em. One man can move quicker than your army."

"Two," said Darnley, loosening his Colts in their holsters. He grinned.

"Two, then," Fargo said. "Get a machete and come on. Tell your men to follow quick as they can."

"Right!" The Englishman barked orders, seized a blade. Then he plunged into the jungle. "Come on, Fargo!"

They both knew the rain forest. They went at a high lope, hacking vines, chopping lianas, whittling through bamboo thickets. They were headed downhill toward a kind of basin. They followed its rim, slithering quickly and silently through the forest like two wild animals, mowing down what lay before them.

The gunfire grew louder.

Fargo, sweating gallons, hacked a vine that bled water freely. He drank from its pouring end, moved on. The people in the valley were giving good account of themselves, and the attackers, probably led by some amateur bandit who had just got his first repeating rifle last week, were bunched out front. That would make it easier.

An hour; now the rifle fire of the attackers was somewhere to their right. Fargo unslung the double-barreled gun, the ideal weapon for this sort of combat. He looked at the perspiration-drenched Darnley, and that wolf's grin tugged his pale lips again.

"All right, Darnley, we're on their flank. Let's go in."

"Yes, by Jove," said Darnley, drawing both guns. "Let's."

Now they abandoned their machetes. As they slithered through the brush and cane like snakes, the ground rose steeply. The higher they came, the less jungle there was. Suddenly they had reached the forest's edge; Fargo halted, staring out at a high rimrock that overlooked a wooded valley. From the last of the cover he and Darnley could see men ranged behind rocks and bushes, firing downward: these were the attackers.

Fargo thumbed extra rounds from the shotgun bandolier, cupped them in his palm. "Let's go," he whispered.

They ran out into the open, low, zigzagging, Fargo with the shotgun leveled, Darnley with a Colt in each hand. The brush came to their knees. Fargo saw a man in white *peon* garb, huge straw sombrero, shirt tied around his belly, skintight pants. He was lying flat, firing into the valley. Beyond him, more were in ragged ranks. The man was so intent on shooting he did not hear or see Fargo coming.

When they were within twenty yards, Fargo jogged to one side. "Take him," he snapped to Darnley and ran to the rear of the line.

He glanced back long enough to see Darnley aim a Colt, pull the trigger. The end man of the line dropped his gun, slumped, the top of his head blown off. Then all hell broke loose.

"*Dios!*" somebody yelled. Men looked

around. They saw Fargo, spotted Darnley, were frozen for an instant. Fargo, in that split second, lined the sawed-off, pulled the right trigger.

Its nine buckshot plowed through the brush. Men screamed as pellets found flesh, ripped in. Up the line, half a dozen others made the mistake of rising, turning, staring at the maker of this unsuspected onslaught. Fargo fired the left barrel, sent nine buckshot hurtling toward them, then dropped breaking the gun as he hit the ground and cramming in new loads.

Overhead, lead whistled. But they were a fraction, a hair, too late. He clicked the Fox shut, pointed it above the brush without exposing himself, sent more shot, eighteen this time, whirring out along the rim as he pulled both triggers.

Rolling frantically, he heard the screams, he knew the loads, deadly as canister, had gone home. He snapped in new shells. Behind him, now, Darnley's Colts were coughing. Fargo risked crawling to his knees.

A thick-bodied man in *peon* clothes, brandishing a Winchester, was on his feet, running forward, brown face contorted. "Here!" he yelled in bastard dialect. "Here, my *bravos*! This is where they're shooting from! Follow me!" Four men sprang up, ran behind him.

Fargo, half erect, lined the shotgun. The thick man saw him, halted dead; the others slammed into him from behind. Then it was too late for all of them. Fargo pulled both triggers.

It was as if they had all run head on into an invisible wall. They fell backward, mowed down like wheat in a writhing, twisting mass. Fargo caught the tang of cordite from the breech as he opened the gun and slugged in new rounds.

He was just closing the Fox again when the bullet caught him.

Fortunately, it was a sharp-pointed, steel-jacketed Mauser. It went clean through his shoulder and kept on going. Even so, it jerked him around like a toy figure, knocked him on his back.

Somebody yelled in triumph, and then they were coming after him. He tried to rise, aim the shotgun, but the shock was too much. He could not lift himself and his shirt was wet. They were going to get him.

Then a pair of booted feet planked themselves beside him. Above his head, as he dropped back, he heard the deep sound of Colts. That, he realized vaguely, was Darnley standing over him, aiming each shot methodically and dropping a man with every one. Somewhere, very far away, men cried out. Then he heard the words: *"Vaya! Vamos! Andale!"* It was a desperate shriek. He heard the sixguns keep on roaring, the sound of galloping hoofs as the bandits mounted and rode. Then there was silence. As Darnley dropped to his knees beside him, Fargo sank back.

"You took one," Darnley said.

"Plug the hole," Fargo rasped. "I'll be all right. Plug the hole and let's go down."

6

CAUTIOUSLY, the two men descended into the Valley of Skulls.

The jungle was dense, towering; but a narrow track led from the rimrock through its green, otherwise impenetrable mass. Fargo, his shoulder expertly bandaged by Darnley with his own undershirt, half a quart of water from the Englishman's canteen in his belly to help replace the blood he'd lost, gained strength instead of losing it from the exertion. His lean, tough body had the resilience of an animal's; more than that, he took a wound like an animal. Once he knew it was minor, he dismissed it, wasted no time on the self-pity and self-coddling that would have kept a lesser man in shock for hours. He moved along briskly as they wound down into the vast basin. Though Darnley urged him to, Fargo would not give up the slung shotgun or the bandoliers, but merely adjusted them so they did not ride the wound.

Still, he was content to trail Darnley, who took the lead, a reloaded Colt in each hand. The big Englishman could move like a stalking cat himself, and neither he nor Fargo made more than a whisper of sound as they passed ever deeper into the valley. Both were wholly alert; the members of the expedition must have perceived that someone had come to their rescue. They were amateurs, and amateurs were always jumpy after battle, inclined to shoot first and ask questions later.

They had made a mile, maybe two, when Fargo touched Darnley's shoulder. The big man froze wordlessly. Fargo moved alongside, pointed. Darnley followed the gesture, nodded.

Ahead and to the right, the wind blew through bamboo that edged the trail. The cane rippled and clacked in the breeze; but there was one spot in its center where the feathery tops moved counter to the wind. Someone was in there, stealing away. Someone, Fargo thought, who did not know much about moving through brush. Likely it was a member of the expedition, but this was no time to take chances.

Darnley grinned. He holstered one Colt, touched Fargo in a signal to wait. Then, silently and fluidly as a snake, he eased into the green wall.

Fargo, the shotgun ready, took cover at the trail side. For five endless minutes the jungle was silent except for the whisper of the breeze in its millions of leaves. Then came the scream.

It was high, shrill, and furious: a woman's cry. The cane whipped, crashed; Fargo tensed as the screaming came closer, as something trampled down the brush. Then, ten, fifteen yards down the trail, Darnley lurched into view, both arms wrapped around a woman who fought like a female jaguar, twisting, biting, kicking.

"All right, lady, all right!" Darnley

laughed, pinioning her arms tightly as she battled him, disregarding the kicking of booted feet against his shins. "We're not going to hurt you, I tell you! We're friends!"

Fargo's mouth twisted in a grin as he saw the blood streaming from Darnley's face where nails like claws had raked it. Darnley came up the trail, holding her clear off the ground. "Blast it, Fargo, give me a hand with this she-cat, will you? I can't let her go for fear she'll take the hide off me."

Fargo stepped out of the brush. "You're Nancy Telford."

Suddenly the girl stopped fighting. Her green eyes widened. "Yes. How'd you know?"

"My name's Fargo. Stoneman's father sent me to you."

For a moment she was motionless, silent; and Darnley did not release her, as if he were enjoying holding her against him. Fargo could understand why. The tight, stained wreck of a white shirt was stretched tautly over full, round breasts; the pants she wore hugged curved hips and fantastic legs. Her hair was an uncombed, tangled, coppery mass, tumbling over her face; those eyes were huge fiery opals, her nose was straight, cleanly chiseled, her lips red and lush. She was a woman made for love, for enjoyment, and she looked out of place in this howling wilderness.

Her gaze roved over Fargo. Then she said, angrily, "Why didn't this big brute tell me that in the first place?"

Reluctantly, Darnley released her. She stood there, magnificent in her fury, breasts rising and falling, eyes glowing. "You didn't give me a chance," said the Englishman. "We saw you moving in the brush, had no way of knowing if you were friend or foe, and I took you. From then on it was fight, not talk." He stepped aside looking at her ruefully, rubbing the streaming clawmarks on his face. "Some thanks, I must say, for coming to your rescue."

"Then you were the ones who drove

off those bandits? You got here just in time! They hit us early this morning and we all fought them — I can handle a rifle, too. Then, when we heard more firing up there, we were afraid it was reinforcements and fell back and took cover. I was in the brush trying to make it back to camp, when the next thing I knew this big . . . whatever it is . . . landed on me."

"It's named Darnley. Roger Darnley. Where's the rest of your outfit? Your father, Stoneman, Norris?"

"They'll be back at the dig by now. That was where we intended to make our last stand. Come on, I'll show you the way — if somebody will get my rifle out of that bamboo."

Darnley retrieved her Springfield from the cane, and she led them down the jungle trail. "I hope you brought some supplies with you. We had just about run out. We were supposed to be re-supplied from Las Casas, but they say the revolution has broken out again and nothing can get through. We were wondering how we were ever going to get out of here."

Darnley smiled. "You can quit worrying. I've got forty armed men, some Indian *arrieros*, mules, and plenty of supplies not far behind." Fargo did not miss the way his eyes lingered on the girl, and his lips thinned. He'd have to talk to Darnley about her; no point in stirring up premature trouble with young Stoneman by messing with his fiancée. This was going to be a tricky enough operation as it was, if Stoneman and Telford had indeed found the Golden Gun.

Then Fargo stopped dead, swung up the shotgun. "Hold it," he whispered.

The others stopped, listened. Ahead, around a bend, there were footsteps on the trail running toward them. Then a voice called, softly: "Nan! Nan! Where the devil are you, Nan?"

The girl smiled. "You can relax. It's Father and Ned."

"Answer them," Fargo said. "We don't want them getting trigger-happy."

"Here I am," she called. "I'm all

right. I've got people with me. They came to help us."

Then the two men rounded the bend, stopping short at the sight of Fargo and Darnley with the girl. Both were armed. Instinctively, the younger one raised his rifle. "Who the hell are you?" he rasped.

Like father, like son, Fargo thought. Ned Stoneman, Jr., was the old man with nearly fifty years peeled away. The same cold blue eyes, the same great hawk's bill of a nose, the same small, pursy mouth. He was six feet tall, rangy, burnt dark with weather; and, Fargo thought immediately, altogether dangerous, a man to be watched. You could almost smell it — the utter ruthlessness, the arrogance, embodied in that muscular frame.

"My name's Neal Fargo," he said; and he told them who they were and what they were doing here.

"Thank God," the older man beside Stoneman said. He was in his early fifties, his hair silvered, his handsome face lined, his body leaned down by the hard work of excavation and the privations of the jungle. He was a strong man, too, Fargo guessed; had to be to venture into regions like this, live and work in them. There was none of the hard, self-centered willfulness in him that made Stoneman so dangerous. "We were at the end of our string. We've done all we can this season; now the important thing is to get what we've uncovered safely out. This is the most valuable archeological find anyone has made so far. Fargo, I think we've found the key to the ancient Mayan language!"

"Oh?" Fargo realized the significance of that. He had seen plenty of Mayan picture writing in his time, knew that until now it remained a mystery; locked up within it was a key to an entire lost civilization, a whole era of history. More than that, if a way could be found to translate the hundreds of examples of it already known, what undiscovered cities and hidden treasures of gold, silver, jade would be thus revealed? Somewhere in the jungle, doubtless, were hidden Mayan caches that would make the Golden Gun seem worthless by comparison! But, "Good," was all he said.

"We've got to get it out," Telford went on. "Back to civilization where it can be studied. You've got mules?"

"Two dozen of them," Fargo said.

Telford looked disappointed. "We could use a hundred, but two dozen will have to do. We can take out the most important objects, anyhow. The stone tablets that hold the key to the Mayan language."

"It'll take all the mules to haul those?"

"Every one of them." Telford turned. "Isn't that right, Ned?"

Fargo's eyes shuttled to Ned Stoneman. The man's face remained impassive. "Yes," he said. "That's right."

"Wait a minute," Darnley said. "You mean you haven't — ?" Just in time Fargo nudged him into silence.

Stoneman looked at the big Britisher. "Haven't what?" he asked tonelessly.

"Nothing," Darnley said. "I was just surprised that a few bloody pieces of rock were considered so damned valuable."

"They are to science," Telford said. "To the science of archeology, to historians, those 'few bloody pieces of rock' are worth a hundred, a thousand times their weight in gold."

Darnley looked at Fargo with something of dismay. Almost imperceptibly, Fargo cautioned him with a motion of his head. He thought he knew what was happening here, but until he was certain, he intended to play his hand cautiously. "Look," he said. "All that can wait. I've got a bullet hole in my shoulder. It don't take long in this climate for a wound to go bad. You've got first-aid supplies, Dr. Telford?"

"Yes, plenty."

"Then suppose we get along, down to the Valley of Skulls. We'll make our plans to get out of here later on."

"That's a good idea," Ned Stoneman said, looking at Darnley and Fargo inscrutably. "Come on." He took Nancy Telford's arm and turned and struck out down the path.

A quarter of a mile along, it dropped steeply, widened. Then they turned a corner and Fargo stopped short.

He had been in a lot of places in his time and he had seen many things counted marvels by ordinary men. But not even he had ever seen anything like this before.

Below them, the ground was scooped out in a huge, natural bowl a mile across. All that area had been cleared of jungle with an immensity of labour that staggered Fargo. But it was not that feat of incredible work and hardship that made him suck in his breath. It was what stood in the center of that clearing.

The pyramid was broad at the base, a full quarter of a mile square, stepped up gradually to a height of nearly a hundred feet; and the stone building on its flattened crest was enormous, sprawling, of heavy blocks of granite. In its center was a granite tower nearly fifty feet high. Even from this distance, looking down upon that huge structure, Fargo could see the carvings on nearly every surface:

fantastic figures of thick-bodied men and women, serpents, even things that looked like elephants, all done to great scale. This, he thought, with a prickling of the short hair on the back of his neck, was a ghost city, the remnants of what had been a thriving metropolis in the very heart, the gut, of impenetrable jungle.

For, all across the clearing and on into the forest beyond, the remains of the huge settlement around the temple on the pyramid were clearly visible: roofless houses of the same granite blocks, some with stucco facing, molded, carved in the same fantastic ornamentation. Once, perhaps fifteen or twenty thousand people had lived here in pride and glory, considering themselves invincible and immortal, their race the greatest ever created by the Gods. Now they were gone, all gone, their vaunted civilization with them. All that remained of their prideful lives were these mute, carved stones. It was incredible, somehow eerie and wholly fascinating. Fargo understood at once Telford's obsession with it, what had brought him to risk his life on such an expedition. It was not so much the drive for scientific knowledge as the impulse that drives treasure seekers. This was indeed a treasure that Telford had uncovered: something the world had never seen since the days of the Spanish conquest. For a moment, looking down at all that, Fargo forgot the Golden Gun. Compared to that spectacle laid out before him, it became a thing of insignificance.

"My God," he said. "You cleared all this yourself?"

"With Indians, yes. Until . . . " Telford glanced at Stoneman, " . . . they ran off, deserted us." He smiled. "It wasn't as difficult as it looks. Mostly, we had to cut back the jungle. In a few places — there was no help for it, though I abhor doing it — we had to blast. But time was short, and fortunately we had plenty of powder. But, you see. You see now why it's so important to get the *stelae*, the great stone tablets with the secret of the writing on them, back to civilization,

131

where scholars can study them. Fargo, this is only one of many cities like this. The Mayan language holds the clue to perhaps ten, fifteen, a hundred more; who can say? And who knows what else lies buried in them? Down there, believe me, are sculptures of men riding elephants. And yet, we have no record of elephants in America at that time. Where did they come from? Why did they cut elephants into stone here in the Mexican jungle? The whole history of man in North America may be revised and altered by what we've discovered here." His eyes shone with a fanatical gleam. "Thank God you've come; thank God for Mr. Stoneman's interest, so we can take a record of all this back. You're not only serving us, you're serving the entire scientific world by coming to our rescue."

"Yeah," Fargo said. Darnley, who shared his awe, was staring open-mouthed at the fantastic spectacle of the lost city below. "Well, when can we load and start?"

"At once," said Telford. "As soon as your men and mules get here. Our work is finished; now there's not a moment to waste in getting its results back to the outside world." Suddenly he laughed. "I'm an idiot, standing here rattling while you've got a bullet hole in your shoulder. Come on, we'll fix you up right away."

A curl of smoke rose from one of the roofless buildings. They threaded their way through the streets of the lost city, in which vines were already beginning to grow again, the incredibly lush jungle already reaching out to reclaim its own. Then they turned through a carved doorway into the shell of what had once been a kind of palace, its rooms, corridors, one upon the other, stretching out with seeming endlessness. Within, tents had been pitched, canvas flies spread to shield equipment and mosquito-barred hammocks.

"The Maya never learned the secret of the arch or the vault," Telford said as

133

they entered. "Consequently, they built their roofs of wood and thatch, and they've all long since rotted." Then, as a small, middle-aged man with a pot belly arose from the fire he had been tending, he went on: "This is my assistant, Mr. Norris. He's been with me for years. He's invaluable."

Norris took Fargo's hand as Telford explained who the newcomers were. Fargo dismissed him instantly as inconsequential; he was no fighter. More, Fargo guessed, camp flunky and general handyman. Then Telford got out his first-aid kit. "Let me see to that shoulder."

They stood around him as he peeled off his blood-sodden shirt. Telford went to work on the wound. Though it hurt, Fargo stood silently and did not flinch. He was more interested in the way Nancy Telford's green eyes ranged over his muscular, battle-scarred torso as her father wrapped gauze. Something gleamed, swirled, deep within those eyes; and her breasts rose and fell beneath her shirt; and he knew then that though she might be engaged to Ned Stoneman, she was not in love with him. Not enough to keep her from grabbing something better if it came within her reach.

He glanced covertly at Stoneman. He had noticed, too, how Nancy's eyes raked over Fargo; and his lips were pursed, his blue eyes even harder. He did not like that, Fargo thought; he did not like that one damned bit. He was a man who, like his father, bought and paid for things and then possessed them wholly with no intention of sharing. Fargo's dislike for Stoneman grew. He had already gleaned from Telford's conversation that the Golden Gun might be here, but Telford had no idea that at least six of the precious mules would be used to haul it out. Apparently Stoneman had not made an issue of that as yet. But, now that the mules were here, he would. Then Telford would learn that he had been betrayed.

Fargo's mouth twisted slightly, but not with the pain of the wound. Currents and crosscurrents. Telford; Stoneman; Darnley; the girl; and himself. Trouble in the air like the tang of gun-powder . . .

Then it was done. As Telford tied the gauze they heard sounds up the trail. "My men," Darnley said. "I'll go meet them." He went out of the shell of the place.

Fargo pulled the bloodstained shirt back on, picked up his bandoliers, started to sling them. "That won't do your wound any good," Telford said.

"I'd rather have a wound than be caught short of ammunition." He looped them into place, then lit a cigar. The smoke tasted good after the ordeal of the treatment. "All right," he said. "We're agreed we're not going to linger here. We'll rest tonight, pull out tomorrow morning. I want to see exactly what we've got to load." He shot a glance at Stoneman. Might as well force the man's hand now and get it over with.

"We've got a lot of *stelae*. We've built carts to transport them with. They're too heavy for one mule to haul. Come, I'll show you." Telford gestured and Fargo followed. Stoneman remained where he was, face impassive. That baffled Fargo.

Was Darnley wrong? Maybe they had not found the Golden Gun. All right, it made no difference; not if these *stelae* were what Telford claimed them to be. They would reveal the secret of other treasures . . .

Telford led him through the labyrinths of the palace. In one great topless room, the *stelae* were spread out — great stone slabs, dozens of them, carved, embossed. Telford's voice rang with pride, excitement. "There, you see? Each divided into two parts. Above, the Maya inscription; below, the translation. Every one of these is a potential Rosetta Stone, Fargo!"

"What's a Rosetta Stone?"

"It was the stone inscribed in both Egyptian hieroglyphics and Greek that enabled a French scholar to decipher the old Egyptian picture-writing. This is the same."

Fargo looked down at the slabs. "That's not Spanish on the bottom."

"No. Latin. The priests. They always moved out first, even ahead of the Spanish soldiers. Some Franciscan must have penetrated this jungle, gained the confidence of the Maya, learned their writing, persuaded them to inscribe these monuments both in their own language and the language of the Church. That's why they're so invaluable, Fargo: absolute treasures of science. And only two dozen mules. We'll be able to haul out nothing but the bare minimum . . . " He shook his head.

The question rose on Fargo's lips then: "What about the Golden Gun?" But he had no time to voice it. Outside the ruined palace there was the jingle and squeak of gear, the clop of mules' hooves, the sound of many voices. Darnley's Raiders had come in.

7

WITH the arrival of the men, Darnley, needing no instructions from Fargo, put out strong guard details around the ruined city. Then, in the gathering twilight, he joined Fargo, Telford and Stoneman in the room of the ruined palace. The girl cooked them supper. All around them, as twilight settled, the jungle literally howled. Monkeys and birds screamed. In the distance a female jaguar in heat unleashed a ghastly cry of yearning that was like the agonized lament of a lost soul. Fargo drank coffee, savored his cigar. The others sat around him on blocks of stone.

"First," he said, "I want to know what happened to all your Indians. You must have had a swarm of 'em to uncover this city. Now they're all gone. You say deserted. Why?"

Telford frowned, hesitated. "Is that important?"

"You're damned right it is. Everything's important in a deal like this. We can't go back out through Chiapas. We've got to haul through the Lacándon, then on through Guatemala into British Honduras. Stoneman's yacht's to meet us there. That forest is full of Indians, and their attitude toward us is damned crucial. Why did they run out? Didn't you pay 'em? Or was it superstition?"

"We paid them," Telford said. "Quite promptly and fully. Superstition — yes, we had some trouble about that. Most of them were latter-day Maya. This was a sacred place to them — especially the Temple up there. They were . . . reluctant to work and — "

"And they had to be forced," Stoneman said harshly.

Fargo looked at him. "Forced?"

"I had to make examples out of some of them, the lazy bastards!"

Fargo took his cigar from his mouth. "What do you mean, examples?"

Before Stoneman could answer, the girl, Nancy, stood up from the fire, came forward. "I'll tell you what he means. He . . . "

"Shut up," Stoneman said.

"No." There was anger in her voice. "You wouldn't listen. We tried to stop you and you wouldn't listen and . . . " She whirled to face Fargo, and now he knew the reason for that roving eye of hers. Whatever she had felt about Stoneman before they had come here, in this place she had seen him plain with the veneer stripped off. And now she doubted; she did not like what he had revealed of himself. "When they refused to work on the temple, he horsewhipped two of them! When they still held out . . . " her voice shook " . . . he shot another one. And when that didn't move them, he . . . hanged one."

"Hanged one?" Fargo's voice rasped as he stared at Stoneman.

"Hell, it got the job done! They cleared the Temple, didn't they? It's the only treatment they understand; it's how they

141

deal with them in the *monterías*, the way my old man used to deal with them when he was fighting down here!"

"Oh, yes, it got the job done!" said Nancy fiercely. "Got it done so well they all just left one night. We went to sleep; the next morning they were gone, every one!"

Fargo felt a sudden coldness. "When was that?"

"Not long ago. A week . . . "

Darnley let out a long breath, already understanding. He got to his feet, turned to Stoneman. "You stupid shit," he said brutally, voice ringing with disgust. "Don't you know they'll be back?"

Stoneman blinked, face reddening. He sprang up. "Now, listen, you . . . "

Darnley smiled coldly, dropped one big hand to a holstered Colt. "You listen. The Maya. They're a pinched-off bit of a noble race, run to seed, true. But that doesn't mean they have no guts. You desecrate a temple they held sacred, you horsewhip some, kill some more — do you think they'll take that lying down? Not bloody likely!" He threw out his other hand in a sweeping gesture. "They're out there now in that jungle somewhere, waiting for their chance. They'd probably have been on you before if those Mexicans hadn't come, attacked you. When the bandits didn't do the job, they'll see that it's done themselves. And now we'll have to fight them all the way across that damned jungle . . . " He turned away contemptuously. "Fargo, I'm doubling the guard."

"Good idea," Fargo said. While Darnley called over one of his lieutenants, snapped orders, he went on. "Now, listen, all of you. My job — and Darnley's is — is to get you out of here in one piece with whatever we can take. That means that from now on, I'm in charge. If anything happens to me, then Darnley takes over. I'll give the orders and there'd better be no questions asked. If there are — " His eyes met Stoneman's, locked with them.

Stoneman shook his head. "My father

hired you. He's paying the freight. You take orders from me."

Fargo grinned coldly. "I take exactly one order from you. My deal with your old man was that you were to have the say on what we haul out. When you've done that, you're finished. You do what I say from then on, or I might give you a little dose of what you gave the Maya."

For a moment, then, the stone enclosure was silent. Criss-crossed with bandoliers, their brass cartridges gleaming in the firelight, draped with shotgun and Winchester, Fargo stood loosely, legs wide-spread. If Stoneman made a move, he thought, a little gunwhipping would be well in order. Might as well show him who was boss from the first. Fargo half hoped Stoneman would make a move; something about the man set his teeth on edge; to work him over with the Colt barrel would be a pleasure.

Then Stoneman yielded; his eyes shuttled away. "I'll discuss this with my father when we get out, don't you think I won't."

Fargo laughed softly. "Talk to him 'til you're blue in the face, I don't care." Then he was all business again, gray eyes hard as rock. "Now. We start loading first thing in the morning. We're pulling out as fast as we can. Six of those mules we need for grub, supplies. That leaves eighteen to haul the stuff from here. Some of these we're gonna lose on the way. So you two — " he looked from Stoneman to Telford — "had better pick and choose what's more important."

"The *stelae* . . . " Telford began eagerly. Stoneman cut in, face flushed.

"The hell with the *stelae*," he said bluntly. "You know what we're hauling. It'll take six mules to pull it."

Telford bit his lip. "But, Ned, the *stelae* are immensely valuable. Every one that we can haul ought to be brought out. The interests of science . . . "

"I don't care about the interests of science!" Stoneman snapped. "I'm here to protect the interests of Ned Stoneman, Senior! You know what the bargain

145

was, Telford! Don't try to weasel out of it now."

The archeologist stood tensely. "Ned," he pleaded, "be reasonable. When I dealt with your father we all assumed that there'd be no trouble getting mules to haul out everything we found! We didn't know we couldn't go the short, easy way back, through Chiapas. We didn't know revolution would break out again! We didn't know either that we'd find such immensely valuable *stelae*, something to revolutionize the whole history of the New World! For God's sake, man . . . I know the other thing is valuable. But when you come right down to it, it's just curiosity. These stone tablets . . ."

Stoneman spat into the fire. "Save your breath, Nelson. Fargo told you the terms of the deal he made with my old man. I pick what's to go and nobody else has a say. And I say we take the other thing. You can haul what *stelae* you can on any mules left over. But on the way, if we lose animals, we'll dump your damned rocks if we

146

have to to save the other thing; *it comes first!*"

Telford's face twisted, almost as if he were about to cry. Then he relaxed, accepted. "Very well. As you say. Remember, though, the agreement *I* made with your father. Really, all this belongs to the Museum at Mexico City. But since things are so unstable, we take it all to the Smithsonian and they hold it in trust until Mexico has a legitimate government again and can be trusted to accept and care for it."

"You can do that with your *stelae*," Stoneman said. "The other, though, goes to Ned Stoneman, Senior, for his private collection."

Telford's face went blank. "That was not in the agreement."

"Maybe you didn't understand the agreement. You do business with my old man, you'd better damned well make sure you understand everything he says. If you don't, you're out of luck."

"But . . . " Telford chopped the air

with his hand in a gesture of frustration. "Ned . . . "

The girl stepped forward. She had combed her hair; it gleamed sleek and coppery in the firelight. Her eyes blazed. "Ned," she said tautly, "do you know what you mean by what you're saying? We . . . we had something once, but you're killing it. You've killed a little bit of it every day we've been here; and now you're just . . . " her voice broke. "You're just wiping the rest of it out."

Stoneman looked at her steadily. "I can't help that," he said in a voice utterly toneless and indifferent. He gestured toward the temple. "I came here to get something and take it back to my father. That's more important to me than anything. You understand? *Anything*!"

Her breasts rose and fell beneath the tight shirt. "Yes," she said at last, thinly. "I understand now. When we met in Madrid, you used me. You made love to me to find out what my father had learned from the old codex. You didn't care about me. You cared . . . all you cared about was *that*." And she pointed to the temple, too. "All you ever wanted, really, was the Golden Gun!"

The Golden Gun: those words spilled out into silence broken only by the crackling of the fire, the shriek of jungle animals. Darnley made a noise in his throat, looked at Fargo in triumph. Stoneman's face contorted; Fargo tensed. For a moment it seemed he'd lash out at her. Then he relaxed, grinned almost mockingly. "All right, you spilled the beans, didn't you? Well, no matter. They would have seen it in the morning."

"You *have* found the Golden Gun?" Fargo snapped.

"You know about it, eh?" Stoneman turned to him.

"I know about it."

"Yeah. Yeah, we found it. This was where they made their last stand, those old Spaniards. From that temple up there, the sacred place. How the hell they got it up there I don't know, but we dug it out from under pile after pile of skulls. It was a good place for a last stand — until they ran out of gunpowder."

Fargo looked toward the vast, imposing bulk of the pyramid. "It's up there now?"

"Clean as a pin, just like the day it was cast. I've had a carriage made for it. Tomorrow we'll bring it down and mount it. And it goes out with us." His eyes glittered. "Do you understand? No matter what or who we have to leave behind, the Golden Gun goes out!"

Fargo nodded. "That's up to you, under my agreement with your father."

Telford let out a despairing sigh. Fargo looked at him, smiled. "Relax, Dr. Telford. It ain't all that bad."

"What do you mean?"

"This. Any *stelae* we leave here are safe. Neither the Indians nor the bandits give a cuss about 'em; to them they're just so much rock. They've lain here hundreds of years already; they'll last a while longer if you cache 'em properly. Then, when things have quieted down, you can come back for them. But the gun — that's another matter. Stoneman's right in this; this is the last chance to get it out. Leave it behind and the vultures will snatch it up and melt it down before you can snap your fingers. Then it'll be gone — forever."

Telford nodded slowly, resignedly. "Yes. Yes, I suppose that's true. Very well. I won't protest further. The gun goes with first priority. But we've *got* to get out some *stelae*, the most important."

"We'll do the best we can," Fargo said. "We'll . . . " He broke off, listening, head cocked. Then he looked at Darnley. "You hear that?"

Stoneman blinked, as Darnley nodded grimly. "I don't hear anything," Stoneman said.

Fargo unslung the shotgun. "That's just it." All at once the jungle, so loud, so full of life, had gone dead quiet. No monkeys chattered or whooped; no nightbirds screeched.

Darnley dropped his hand to his Colts. "Well," he said, "they're out there!"

"Who?" Stoneman's voice was hoarse.

"Your little friends," answered the Englishman. "The ones with debts to collect from you. The Maya, Stoneman — the Indians."

Stoneman stood frozen for a moment. Then he snatched up his Springfield rifle. "All right," he grated. "Let the bastards come! We beat the Mexicans, we'll teach them a lesson, too!"

"Put that Goddamned gun down!" Fargo snapped.

Stoneman shook his head angrily. "No! Do you think I'm afraid of them — ?"

Fargo laughed coldly. "You'd sure as hell better be. You're the one they want. If they get hold of you, it'll take you a long time to die." Then his face was grim. "Maybe the best thing to do would be to give you to them as a peace offering. Then they'd go away and leave us."

"You wouldn't . . . " Stoneman paled.

"I might, if push came to shove," said Fargo tersely. "How many Indians did you have working here, Telford?"

"Nearly fifty."

"All from the same village?"

"No. From several."

"Then we've got trouble," Fargo said. "My guess is there's more than a hundred, maybe two hundred of them out there. They're normally pretty peaceful people, but there's only so much even they will take."

"So what the hell? We've got nearly fifty guns. They won't come in against all that. If they did, we could cut them down like flies."

"Here, yes," said Fargo. "In the open. But we're not going to be hauling that gun and the rest through the open, Stoneman. We're going to be taking it through the jungle." He pointed. "*Their* jungle." His mouth twisted.

"They're not *Ladinos*, Stoneman — mestizos, half-castes who're as afraid of the jungle as any white man. They're forest Indians, born and bred here. They can hunt us all along the trail and pick us off one by one with poisoned arrows. We'd never even see anything to shoot at."

"Then what do we do?" For the first

time, Stoneman's voice shook a little.

"We parley with them. That Golden Gun. You say you've cleaned it up?"

"Yes."

"Bore, touch-hole, all? It could be fired?"

"Fired?" Stoneman said blankly.

"Damn it, that's what it was made for, wasn't it?" Fargo went to the corner of the room, threw back the big tarp that covered supplies. He made a sound of satisfaction as he saw the cans of blasting powder, the coil fuse. "Darnley."

The big Englishman was beside him in a moment. "Right, Fargo."

Fargo handed him two cans of powder, a rope of fuse. "Climb the pyramid, up in the temple. Get to that gun. Remember, it wasn't made to hold modern powder, so don't use too big a load. Charge it, wad it, no projectile of any kind, and give a yell when you're ready. Fire four times, once in each direction. Take men with you to help turn the gun; plenty of men." He began to strip off his bandoliers, laid aside his own weapons. "All right,

Stoneman, I want money. Gold, hard cash. You must have brought in plenty with you to pay the workers."

"Now, wait a minute. You're not going to pay those lousy animals tribute . . . "

"I'm going to pay 'em compensation for the men you killed, men who were support of families. I hope that will calm them down. Then, if everything goes right, I'm going to scare the living hell out of 'em."

"Don't be a fool! We can hole up in the temple, it's sacred to them, they're scared to death of it, won't go near it. That's why I had to force them . . . "

"Oh, sure. We could hole up there. We wouldn't be the first, either, would we? Remember the Spaniards? You want to wind up like them?" Fargo unbuckled his cartridge belt. "Give me the damned money. And all the tobacco you've got in camp, you must have had a supply for them."

"We've got plenty," Nancy Telford said quickly. "But — " Her voice trembled. "Fargo, you're not going out there unarmed, to try to talk with them?"

"I'm going to make a stab at it," Fargo said. He turned, giving Darnley more instructions. "Twenty minutes," he said. "You got it? Exactly twenty minutes. Get on the bit; you've got no time to lose. The money, Stoneman — "

Reluctantly, Stoneman unbuckled a money belt from beneath his shirt, handed it to Fargo. "They'll kill you and take the whole damn thing — "

"Don't judge other people by yourself," Fargo said thinly. "They've got a grudge to settle, yes. If it can be settled to their satisfaction, they'll keep their word. If it can't . . . Well, if they come at you, fight like hell." He threw the belt over his shoulder. Then, with no weapon but the Batangas knife, he turned to go, seizing up a long brand from the fire to use as a torch.

"Fargo," Nancy Telford said.

He glanced at her. "Yes?"

Her eyes shone. "Be careful."

"Always am," he said, then went out.

What the others did not realize, Fargo thought as he walked across the silent clearing through the shadows of the ruined buildings, was that the jungle out there was full of Indians — not just these, but hundreds, thousands, more along their line of march. The killing of two had brought two hundred in a quest for vengeance; those two hundred could conceivably be killed, but then two thousand would seek to avenge them. No; this had to be tried first, if it were not to be a running fight they could not afford or hope to win all across the Lacándon, hampered by a ton of gold and more hundreds of pounds of stone.

He checked his watch, quickened his pace. Timing was important, all important. He loped across the clearing, holding the torch high and knew the Indians would see it moving toward them and wonder at it. When he reached the clearing's edge, he slowed, held up the torch in his left hand, and raised his right high, palm out, in the signal for peace.

Ahead of him loomed the forest wall,

night-shrouded, black, impenetrable, utterly silent. The torchlight cast a yellow, flickering glow on the thick greenery of the jungle. Within that growth, behind that wall, nothing moved, made sound, or stirred. And yet, they were there; undoubtedly they were there.

Now, very slowly he went forward, eyes searching the rim of forest. His whole body was tense; it would be no trick at all for gun or arrow fired from cover to kill him. Curiously, he felt no fear; he thought he knew the Indians too well. He was a stranger to them and came in peace; they had no grudge against him and they would at least talk to him — he hoped.

He knew none of their dialects — or not more than a few words — but he was fluent in Spanish. Of course, some of them must speak it; surely the headman who had dealt with Telford and Stoneman. He stopped ten feet out of the jungle. Then he called out boldly and steadily in Spanish: "Friends. Maya. Lacándon. I come in peace to talk."

No answer. The night seemed to hold its breath. Nothing stirred.

But he could feel them in there, in the jungle; sensed, with an instinct like an animal's, their presence. "My name is Fargo. I would talk with the leader of the Maya."

Again a wait. Then, for the first time, there was the audible stir of life within the brush. Fargo held the torch high, right hand up. "I am unarmed. I would talk."

Time was ticking away. And time was precious. Everything had to go exactly right. Damn it, he thought — Then the answer came.

"I am called Sabino," the voice said in rusty Spanish. "I am headman of my tribe. I would talk with the man called Fargo." Shadows moved along the jungle wall. Then they were there. Five of them, some in loin cloths, two in dirty whites. Sabino was one of these, stepping forward, a man of middle age, thick, stocky, and impressive. He carried an ancient muzzle-loading musket, its pan primed, hammer cocked, and flint ready, and the bore of the thing was pointed at Fargo's belly. The others were armed with guns of equal antiquity. They ranged around Fargo; he saw other movement in the jungle and knew that he had under-estimated the number of Indians out there; the place swarmed with them.

"I know why the Maya are here and ready for war," Fargo said. "There have been evil things done to the Maya by the man, Stoneman."

"Yes. We have come for him. Two families are fatherless because of him. Blood seeks blood . . ."

"I will deal with Stoneman," Fargo said. "I am a *Norteamericano* who will see that Stoneman is punished. I have in the North a friend who is a great chief, who loved the Indian and who hates the man who does injustice to them. He will see that Stoneman is punished in the ways of his own people."

Sabino stared at him impassively. Then he spat. "That puts no food in the mouths of crying children."

"Neither does a Maya knife in Stoneman's belly. But this will." Fargo unslung the money belt. He opened one compartment, took out a handful of gold, held it high, let the coins dribble through his fingers in a yellow shower, fall to the earth in a pile.

Even Sabino, despite his Indian impassiveness, gasped at the sight of so much wealth. Two hundred dollars in gold, probably, Fargo guessed; and that would be more cash than an entire Indian village saw in a decade.

"This will feed the hungry children. It will buy new guns for the village with which to hunt. New tools with which to till your *milpas*. And if you have sons or brother enslaved in the *monterías*, this will buy them free."

It was a good bet that they did; few Indian villages were without those unfortunates who had borrowed from money-lenders and were doomed to work themselves to death in the logging camps in repayment of the debt. Five or ten dollars American were the enormous sums they owed — and which they could never earn back to buy their freedom.

Sabino made a sound in his throat. "The Maya," Fargo went on, "are entitled to this for their dead men." He unsnapped another compartment. "And this," he added, as a second stream of gold as large as the first trickled through his fingers.

"So much," he said. "And my promise that Stoneman will face my great chief's justice in his own homeland."

Sabino licked his lips, stared down at the gold.

"This is something strange. That a white man should come before us unarmed when there are so many guns in camp. That he should give us gold, which white men hate to part with . . ."

"The Gods so want it," Fargo said. He searched his memory for a word, a Mayan word he'd heard somewhere in his travels, the single random name of a Mayan God. Somehow it had something to do with that temple back there. Then it came to him. "The ancient ones desire it. Especially *Multuntzekil.*"

Sabino jerked up his head at the name. "*Multuntzekil? Lord of the Heaps of Skulls?* What know you of him?"

Fargo pointed. "His temple is there."

"Yes. But . . . "

"In a moment, he will speak."

"Speak?" Their eyes widened, they looked at each other in the torch light, open-mouthed.

"Yes. In flame and thunder *Multuntzekil* speaks. To tell you I speak truth. We want only to leave this place, to leave the sacred Mayan temple and the sacred skulls. To go in peace. *Multuntzekil* will say that to you . . . " Fargo thumbed out his watch, stole another glance. Four minutes, if Darnley followed schedule. "Will you take the money and let us go?"

Sabino hesitated. He seemed on the verge of consent; and then another Indian shoved into the torchlight; and suddenly Fargo realized that here was trouble. This one was younger, his black eyes sharp, glittering, his mouth a wide, bitter, impatient slit. "The old gods are dead!" he snapped. "The white men have killed them! They no longer speak!" He held a machete high, as if ready to slash. "The white man Stoneman has beaten me with his whip. He will not do that to me or anyone again!" He spat. "We take the money. But we take the white men, too. I, Chan Ka, say that."

"The white men have guns," he said. "Many guns. More will die."

"This one has no guns!" Chan Ka rasped. He took another step forward, drew back the machete. "And as for the others — are we women?" A second more and that blade was coming down . . . Fargo tensed.

"Wait!" Sabino's voice halted it. "I am still headman here." He touched the gold with his foot. "We have no quarrel with this one, he came unarmed, in peace — and this is fair payment for our wrongs. You shall have your share. Enough to buy your brother back from the *montería* at Agua Azul. Why should

164

more women weep?" He stared at Fargo. "We will hear the voice of *Multuntzekil*, Lord of the Heaps of Skulls. You say he will speak. Never in my knowledge has he done so before. But, now — prove what you say, white man. Prove it to Chan Ka and to me and the others."

Fargo licked dry lips. He turned slowly. The pyramid bulked black against the sky. Atop it, the ruined temple and its tower was a jumble of silent stone, deeply shadowed. *Damn it, Darnley*, he thought, aware of that machete poised for the swing. *Damn it, you'd better be quick* . . .

"Watch," he said steadily. "Watch and listen. From his temple, the Lord of the Heaps of Skulls will speak in flame and thunder." He raised his voice. *Now*, he thought. "Cry out, oh, Multuntzekil!" he roared.

And, as if in answer, from the temple on the pyramid a huge tongue of flame belched white into the darkness, and just behind it came a clap of thunder. In the silence of the night, the sound was terrific, echoing and re-echoing in the hushed jungle. Then the jungle was no longer silent, but a wild cacophony of frightened birds and animals shrieking and gibbering at the tops of their lungs.

Sabino gasped. He clapped a hand to his open mouth. "He speaks!" he whispered.

"Yes," said Fargo. "He says take the gold and go; leave the white man to the white man's justice."

Chan Ka made a contemptuous sound in his throat, but he was, nevertheless, trembling slightly. Fargo sensed what went on inside him: common sense warring with superstition. As a worker in the camp, he had heard blasting, knew the sound of blasting powder. But at night, with such a tongue of flame, coming from the sacred temple at Fargo's command . . .

"I do not believe it," he rasped in Spanish.

"Speak again, Lord of the Heaps of Skulls!" Fargo yelled that across the clearing. *You'd better have that damned gun turned, reloaded, by now, Darnley* — "Speak — !"

Up there in the ruined temple, flame cleft the darkness once again with brilliant orange-white. Once more, deep and rolling, thunder boomed across the clearing, jarring the very air. The shrieking in the jungle heightened. All that howling and screaming in the brush was eerie, spooky, even to one used to the night noises of the tropics; it was like the scream of souls in torment, the gibbering of demons. All around the clearing now, Fargo saw that Indians had appeared in the open, staring, awe-filled, at the pyramid. Then — Darnley was a quick man with a cannon — the gun roared again.

Fargo turned. Chan Ka had lowered the machete. He stood there trembling, biting his lip. *One more time*, thought Fargo. By turning the gun, Indians on all sides would have a clear look at that white tongue of flame, hear the thunder directed toward them.

The gun fired its final charge. The

thunder rolled and died. Fargo let out a long breath. "You have heard *Multuntzekil*," he said.

"It's only — " Chan Ka began, but his voice was empty of defiance, now; feeble. "It's only — "

"It is the voice of the ancient ones," Sabino whispered. "I never thought to live to hear it." Suddenly he fell to his knees. For a moment, Fargo thought that he was praying. But he was scooping up the gold, cramming it into his pockets.

Chan Ka watched for an instant. Then he was on his knees, too, the machete thrown aside. He seized gold, crammed it in his loin cloth.

"It must be divided!" Sabino snapped. "It must be divided fairly."

"Yes," Fargo said. "The God has said that." His voice was stern, full of authority.

His pockets loaded, Sabino scrambled to his feet.

"We have our justice," he said, staring at Fargo. "The lives of the dead men have brought riches to the rest of us.

That must have been the plan of the ancient Gods for them. In the old days, men were killed here for the same reason, so that the gods would send us wealth. And now, with my own ears, I have heard the God of the Temple of the Skulls speak in thunder and have seen with my own eyes his tongue of fire. And — " He hesitated. "You will leave this sacred place? All of you?"

"By tomorrow night we'll be gone, if you will let us pass safely."

"So be it. Chan Ka?"

The younger one looked at him. As he turned, Fargo could see the half-healed ridges and welts across his back, some of them still infected. Stoneman, Fargo thought tautly, had given him a devil of a beating. In Chan Ka's place, he would have wanted Stoneman's blood and got it, God or no God.

Chan Ka, however, only nodded: "Let them go," he said harshly. "I am content." But he turned, looked toward the temple, and his face was hard.

"Then I will pass the word," said Sabino. He wheeled, snapped something in a soft, liquid dialect like running water — probably Quiché-Maya, Fargo thought. The others nodded, loped off in opposite directions as runners.

"You are free to go," said Sabino. "You will not be harmed. But when the sun has risen twice, you must no longer be in this place."

"We'll not be," Fargo said. "I have brought another present. Tobacco." He handed over the drawstringed sack full of pipe mixture.

Sabino took it gravely, nodded thanks. "We will smoke it to the ancient gods." He turned away. Then, almost magically, he disappeared into the jungle, musket and all, and Chan Ka melted after him.

Fargo let out a long breath. The torch had burned down, was burning his fingers. He dropped it, stamped it out. Then, in darkness, relying on the word of the old Maya, he turned his back and strode, defenseless, away.

Ten minutes later, he had reached the ruined palace.

Darnley was there. He looked at Fargo in the firelight. "You could use a drink," he said, and found a bottle in the supply pile and passed it over. "Did it work?"

"I wouldn't be here if it hadn't," Fargo said thinly. He took a long drink — one he needed as badly as any he had ever swallowed. He passed the bottle to Darnley, turned to Stoneman, Telford and the others. "There'll be no trouble with the Indians if we're out of here in twenty-four hours." Then he threw Stoneman's money belt to the man. "It cost you about four hundred bucks in gold."

"Four hundred dollars?" Stoneman's eyes flared. "Damn you — "

"Shut up," Fargo said quietly, and he reached and got the shotgun. "Just shut up. One more word out of you and I'll give you to them. You understand?"

His eyes bored into Stoneman's, and Stoneman turned away. "All I can say," he grated, "is that you'd better get that cannon out of here and to Belize safe and sound."

"I'll do what I've been paid for," Fargo said.

8

DARNLEY kept a heavy guard posted all night with orders to fire only if fired upon. Thus, since there were no more alarms, Fargo got seven hours badly needed sleep in a hammock beneath a jury-rigged mosquito bar. He and the hole camp were up long before dawn. There was much to be done and it was vital that they keep their promise to the Maya and clear this place before the next day's sunrise.

He was finishing his coffee when Darnley came to stand beside him. "You haven't seen it yet, have you?"

"No."

"Come and look at it. It's a sweet artillery piece. Those old Spaniards knew their business. And that temple — Jove! Something to raise the short hair on your neck."

Fargo drained the cup, set it aside.

"Let's go." He looked around. "Where're the Telfords and Stoneman?"

"Up there." Darnley gestured to the top of the pyramid.

A stair of ancient stone led up its long, sloping side. It was a steep, hard climb. Darnley chuckled. "Damned good thing for you I'm in top shape. Not many men could have made a fast run up this with a can of gunpowder under each arm. And to turn that thing around the way you wanted . . . It took ten of us with iron bars!" He lowered his voice, suddenly serious, nudged Fargo. "You've never seen anything like it, believe me," he whispered. "Fargo, this will be the biggest score anybody's made down here since the days of Sir Francis Drake!"

Then they had reached the top of the pyramid. Above them, the roofless temple hulked. Darnley led him between great piles of stone. Then he stopped short. "There," he said.

Fargo stared.

At the base of the square, stone tower, the skulls were piled. Hundreds of skulls, thousands of them — tribute to *Multuntzekil*. A vast heap, a great mound, they stared at Fargo with crazy, eyeless, tilted sockets, grinning jaws — almost as if mocking the living, full of knowledge denied to those not yet dead. Some were caked with dirt, others cracked and splintered. Dwarfed by that great heap of bone, Fargo could not help a shiver.

"That's not all," said Darnley. "Over here." He led Fargo to a deep hole in the top of the pyramid. "Telford said they found the cannon down here under all those skulls, lying on the rest of them. Look." Fargo stared down into a vast pit. There was no telling how far into the pyramid it extended. It, also, was jammed with skulls. They looked up at him coldly in the gray light of dawn.

"The Maya, of course, had heard the legend of it," Darnley continued. "But they wouldn't touch these skulls; they were too scared, and they ran away before the gun was uncovered. Stoneman and the others lifted it out with a block and tackle. You were lucky last night. If they'd suspected the cannon was up here, they might have guessed what your voice of the Lord of the Heap of Skulls was."

They walked around the rim of the great pit, staring at its gruesome contents. Nelson Telford stood on its far edge, staring moodily down. As they approached he shook his head sadly.

"What's the matter, Telford?" Fargo asked.

"It hurts me," Telford said, "to leave all this unexcavated. Who knows what's down there? Oh, God, if we just had time to move the rest of the skulls. The things we might find in the bottom of that pit — "

"Maybe you can come back someday," Fargo said.

"No." Telford shook his head. "I doubt I ever will. I have a feeling it'll be a long time before Mexico's quiet enough for any other expedition to return here, and I'm too old. Well . . . " He sighed, turned. "If only we can get those *stelae* out . . . "

"The Golden Gun is over here, other side of the tower," Darnley said.

They rounded the pile of stone. There Nancy Telford and Ned Stoneman were in low, intense, angry conversation. "I told you last night," she snapped. "It's off."

"Listen — " Stoneman seized her arm, squeezed. She cried out in pain. Fargo stepped forward.

"Stoneman," he said.

The man turned, still holding Nancy.

"Let her go," said Fargo.

Stoneman stared at him. Then, slowly, he released his hold.

"Don't lay a hand on her again, you understand?" Fargo said.

Something flared in Stoneman's eyes, then died.

"You go on down to camp, Nancy," Fargo ordered, "and get the cooking outfit together, you and Norris."

"Yes," she said, shot a look of disgust and hatred at Stoneman. She rounded the tower rubbing her arm.

"Where's the gun?" Fargo asked.

"There," said Darnley, leading him further around the tower and pointing.

Fargo stopped short, sucking in breath as if someone had hit him in the stomach. He had never seen, never even dreamed of such a thing. The reality of it was awesome.

There it sat, on pinless trunions — a perfect Spanish cannon of pure, soft gold: bell-breeched, bell-mouthed, perhaps twelve feet long and gleaming dully in the light of the sun just rising over the jungle. Two thousand pounds or maybe double that — a weapon and a fortune simultaneously. Now he knew why the legend of it had haunted old Stoneman for decades.

Fargo looked at it in fascination, greed and awe for a long moment. Almost, he was tempted, now — tempted to join with Darnley and take this thing for his own. Then he came back to earth. He had made a bargain with Stoneman. Now the job was to get this golden monster across hundreds of miles of jungle without losing or ruining it.

He lit a cigarette thoughtfully. He did not think the Indians would try to take it from them. It was more than they could cope with, more than they could comprehend. But as it was being transported through the jungle, the Indians would be watching them and were bound to see it. In this land news traveled on the air — seemingly like pollen. The word would reach every *montería*, every trading village and pueblo, every town of any size: an army of *gringos* was transporting through the jungle a gun of solid gold, valuable beyond imagining. Melted down, it could finance an army or buy a man a huge ranch and many women. And they would come . . . the *buscaderos, revolucionarios, pistoleros* . . . they would have to be outrun, out-fought. Fargo ran his hand over the golden cannon. Its long, sleek, soft tube was flawless, devoid of crack or weakness. And this, he thought, would help fight them off. And it must be mounted and ready for action as soon as possible, for the first band could come at any time.

"Let's get this thing down off the pyramid," he said, "and on its carriage. Telford, I have bad news for you."

Telford stared at him. "What?"

"I'm afraid you're going to lose another mule."

"No!" the man exploded.

"Yes. We need it to haul all the gunpowder you've got. And as many round rocks as we can pick up."

Darnley comprehended, grinned. "Going to let it fight its own way out?"

"Wait a minute!" Stoneman snapped. "You mean you're going to use it as artillery?"

"If we have to," Fargo said. "And likely we'll have to."

"No!" Stoneman's face was red. "You can't load and fire it! The heat will melt the gold, ruin the bore: it'll blow up! It wasn't designed for that!"

"I'll serve it," Fargo said. "I can serve any gun that was ever made and serve it right. I won't blow it up."

"I refuse! I won't let you!"

Fargo looked at him for a long minute. Then his hand moved. But no one could see the movement; it was too swift for that. One instant it was at his side; the next, it was out front, the .38 Colt in it centered on Ned Stoneman.

"Listen," Fargo said. "This thing is full of hollow-points. If one of them hits you, it'll tear you wide open. My patience is at an end, Stoneman. The next time you try to give me orders — tell me what to do and what not — I'm going to kill you." His tone left no doubt that he meant exactly what he said.

Stoneman turned pale; his jaw clamped shut. Then the gun was back in Fargo's holster as swiftly as it had come. "I think we understand each other," he said coolly. "Now, let's get to work."

Work. That was what it was . . . hard, back-breaking labor. They cursed and sweated, Darnley's men, Fargo riding them mercilessly, as they slid the huge tube of gold on runners of mahogany down the great pyramid, mounted it on the mahogany carriage Stoneman had already made. That the carriage was a good job Fargo grudgingly admitted, except the rims of the wheels sliced from rounds of great mahogany trunks were too narrow, and that was going to cause trouble in soft ground.

Still, with the wooden trunion bar in place, the gun was nicely mounted. There was a sort of trail that could be spiked in to stabilize while firing . . . if it came to that. Cans of blasting powder, coils of fuse, and big bags of rock fragments were packed on the mules that pulled it. The earliest cannons ever made, Fargo knew, had fired stone projectiles. At close range they could be deadly. A load of rocks fired from the Golden Gun at fifty yards or less would spray like canister or grape, be effective against personnel. Moreover, the gun's roar itself was a factor in their favor: Fargo knew from experience how men hesitated before the sound of artillery.

They were three strong carts for *stelae*. They were loaded with the precious slabs and their mules hitched up; the remaining animals were packed with food and ammunition. Fargo backed off, looked at the packtrain as it strung itself out ready for departure. It was a hell of an outfit to get through jungle, across rivers and past swamps — slow as molasses and awkward as two left feet. And a millstone around a man's neck when the time came to fight. Still, he had hired out to get it to Belize; and he would do his damndest.

The Indian *macheteros* took their place at the column's head. Directly behind them came the Golden Gun. Darnley's men were strung out on either flank, Darnley commanding a strong rear guard. The archeologist and Stoneman would ride the carts or walk beside them when the going was too rough for the mules to pull their added weight. Fargo would take the lead beside the cannon.

He saw that everything was ready. He raised his hand high, then brought it down sharply. "Move out!" he roared.

Whips cracked; a mule brayed. The animals strained into harness. The Golden Gun began to roll. Fargo took one look backward at the lost city, the pyramid, the temple of the Valley of Skulls. Then, with long strides, he took his place in line and the train rolled into the jungle.

The first two days were pure hell. After that, it got worse.

Inch by inch, foot by foot, they fought their way through a green Purgatory, building a road for the vehicles as they went, hacking down cane and vines, corduroying the ground with logs when it turned soft. Then, when the wheels sank in and the cannon and carts mired, they threw their weight against them and adding their strengths to that of the struggling mules to work them free. Meanwhile, the heat was stifling, the insects ferocious. Indians were out there in the jungle, watching.

On the fourth day, they had struck a sort of narrow trail that made the going easier. Now Fargo walked ahead of the *macheteros*, shotgun cradled in his arm, his eyes scanning ceaselessly the ground before him and the jungle that lay ahead. He was so intent on this that Nancy Telford was at his elbow before he realized it. "Fargo," she said.

He held up, looked at her. "Don't ever come up behind me that way again," he said.

"I'm sorry." She frowned. "I just wanted to walk with you. I . . . can't stand being close to Ned. Why're you so jumpy? The going's easier now."

"That's why I'm jumpy. A trail means men can come and go. There'll be other trails feeding into it. When there wasn't any path, we were hard to get at. But we can be got at now. You'd better drop back to the rear."

"No. I want to stay with you. Please." Whether by accident or design — he did not know — she leaned against him and her breast touched him briefly, solidly. His mouth twisted.

185

"Damn it," he said, "you do what I say."

She hesitated. "Very well," she said at last, and fell back. Fargo moved on ahead, more swiftly now. His whole being was focused, concentrated, on reading sign. In the dim, stifling murk of the rain forest, he brought to bear every ounce of experience gained over hard years of combat. Even so, he almost walked into the ambush.

It was his ears that saved him.

At this time of day, except for the occasional riffling of a rare breeze, the animals drowsed in refuge from the heat; the leaves hung down limply as if exhausted; only the omnipresent insects buzzed and whirred. By habit, Fargo stopped every few yards to listen, far enough ahead of the wagon train now so that its sounds did not interfere with his reconnaissance. Now, coming to a point where the narrow trail made a sharp, right-angle turn, he halted, cocked his head. Such a place was one of maximum danger. A man who knew his business would hit a long outfit like this just as its center swung around the curve, when the front was separated from the rear.

So he stood there a long time with head cocked, breath held. Then he caught the sound, faint, brief: the slosh of water. It lasted only a half-second, but that was long enough for him to hear and identify it; and he knew that someone up ahead and around the bend lay in wait and had just shifted position. What he had heard was water moving in a half-empty canteen.

Instantly, he seemed to relax. He knew he was being watched; probably guns were trained on him. But whoever lay hidden up there would not want to fire prematurely, tip his hand. Given no reason to do so, he — or they — would wait until they were sure of their prey.

Fargo tilted back his hat, took out a bandana, mopped his forehead. He slung the shotgun, sighed, sat down at the trail's edge, took out a cigarette, lit it. There was time, plenty of it; the train was far behind, coming at a snail's pace.

He smoked the cigarette through, as if tired and unconcerned and grateful for the break. His ears were straining, but there was no other sound.

All the same, he knew what he had heard. When the cigarette was finished, he arose a little stiffly. He took a leisurely swallow from his canteen, wiped his mouth, and then ambled back down the trail toward the train. The path jogged again; he stepped behind the wall of brush at its bend. Then, like a ghost, he faded into the jungle.

Vines, cane, briars, underbrush: a solid wall through which it seemed not even a snake could pass. Certainly whoever lay up there would not expect a white man, a *gringo*, to come through it so swiftly, deftly and soundlessly. But Fargo was an old hand at this: he found holes where there were no holes, twisted, turned, edged sideways, crawled, and worked his way back toward the origin of that sound with astonishing speed. He was sweating and bloody from a hundred scratches when he halted behind a hung fallen log, the rotted carcass of a jungle giant, crawling with ants and other biting insects that made him grimace as they nipped and stung him. But he endured that pain and made no attempt to fight them off. Instead, cautiously, head low, he peered around the log's butt end; and then he saw them.

On this side of the trail, at least, there were fifteen. Probably as many more across the way. They lay posted at the trail's edge in groups of five, screened by the jungle wall, each group ten yards apart. Their rifles were at the ready and there were pistols at their belts, and he judged that they were the *capos*, the foremen, and their crews of gunmen from some *montería*. They had caught wind of the Golden Cannon, and had let the timber-cutting go while they formed a gang to take it. They were tough and hard and jungle-wise, and they had made only that one mistake. Either they should have kept their canteens full enough not to slosh, or abandoned them altogether.

Fargo grinned, like a hunting wolf.

Then he turned around, went back the way he came. Because he had already found a passage, he made much better time.

Then he had rejoined the train, catching it a hundred yards down-trail from the ambush. He made no attempt to halt it, but he strode rapidly along it toward its rear, and Darnley saw him coming and met him. "What's up?"

Fargo told him. Darnley grinned coldly. "All right. We'll take the bastards from the rear."

"Can't. Jungle's too thick. Couldn't get around behind them."

"What, then?"

Fargo jerked his head, and Darnley's grin widened. The Golden Gun traveled fully charged; at every halt, Fargo himself checked its load. Not too much blasting powder; the gun was not designed to take much strain. Some wadding, then a load of rocks, more wadding. Improvised and rude, but the powder was dry and it would fire.

"Swing most of your men over to the

left. Give me a detail on the right. When I fire, open up into the jungle with everything you've got." He turned, went back up the line. Telford, Norris, Nancy and Stoneman were riding on the carts. "There's going to be shooting," Fargo said briefly and told them of the ambush in a few words. "The four of you keep down behind the *stelae*."

Whatever else he was, Stoneman was no coward. He lifted his rifle. "The hell I will — "

"I told you to do what I say. I took money to bring you out of here." Fargo's hand dropped to his Colt. "But if I have to kill you myself, I will."

Stoneman's face turned red, his eyes glittered, and he bit his lip. "All right," he grunted and let the gun down.

Fargo continued up the line. Some of Darnley's men fell in behind him. The trail here was wide enough so that the *macheteros* loafed along, enjoying their rest. The gun was within fifty yards of the ambush now, its muzzle pointed backward. Fargo walked up beside the off leader of the mules. Without warning, he pulled the team around in the narrow trail. They brayed, plunged, crashed in the brush. The gun swung, and as its muzzle came into line, Fargo reached down to pull the clevis pin that connected it to the harnessed team. "Hold those mules!" he snapped to the teamster and the *macheteros*. He crouched behind the gun and snapped a match and put it to the short fuse already riding in the touchhole. It caught, hissed. At that instant a rifle fired from up ahead as an ambusher saw what had happened. The lead whined off the cannon tube and Fargo jumped back, crouched low, shotgun unslung, and then the Golden Gun went off.

Its thunder shook the jungle, and the cloud of smoke it billowed made a fog. But, at close range, its charge of small rocks crashed into the jungle foliage and mowed it like a scythe. In there men screamed and yelled; at the same instant, Darnley's Raiders opened up on the left, pumping fire at the bend's outside curve.

Taken by surprise, men boiled out of the jungle on both sides of the trail, firing as they came. Fargo's mouth curled as he aimed the shotgun. The charge had flushed no more than eight or nine from the right; the rest of the fifteen had been put out of action by the gun.

Then there was no time to think. They came on fast in that narrow space, and he fired the right barrel of the shotgun straight down the trail, like a ball sent down a bowling alley. The nine buckshot slammed men back with a brutal fist, and those behind fell over them. Fargo fired again, broke the shotgun, crammed in another pair of rounds, snapped it closed. A bullet caught the old campaign hat's peak and whipped it off; another rasped by his ear so close he felt its wind. This time he cut loose with both barrels at once, and the cannon itself could have done no more damage. Chopped, slashed, by that lethal double load, more men went down, and the trail ahead was a writhing, twisting mass of bodies into which Darnley's raiders poured their fire. But there were survivors, and they came on, brave men crazed with greed, the tough *pistoleros* of the logging camps. There was no time to load again; they jumped the corpses of their fellows and, before Fargo could fall back, they were on him. He turned the shotgun, butt first, in his left hand, drew his Colt with his right. A round, swarthy face, sweating, black-mustached, loomed before him, teeth bared; he saw a pistol-muzzle dead on him from three feet away. The upswung shotgun butt knocked it aside as it went off, and the bullet ripped Fargo's cheek. Simultaneously, he fired the Colt. The hollowpoint hit full force into the *pistolero's* face and the whole head disappeared. Fargo himself was sprayed with red and gray as the man dropped, but there was no time to flinch at that. He whirled, but too late; an arm clamped around his neck, squeezed. He rammed the short gun under that arm, muzzle against a flank, fired. Hot breath grunted in his ear; then the arm fell away, the knifeblade in the other hand bouncing off the cartridges of his bandolier.

Mules brayed and kicked; the whole trail seethed with combat; the jungle rang with gunfire, was pungent with powdersmoke. Fargo caught a glimpse of Darnley, sixgun in each hand, firing to the right and left, saw two men go down. But Darnley's men were taking casualties, too. One dropped kicking in the trail; the rearing, plunging mules that teamsters fought desperately to hold trampled him, and his scream faded quickly. Another yelled, dropped, clutching his stomach; a third toppled into the underbrush. Fargo saw a big man, a *montería capo*, ten feet away, raising his rifle, lining it on Darnley. He fired the colt from the hip and the hollow point tore out the small of the *capo's* back and dropped him like a log.

And then, with astonishing suddenness, it was over. All at once the jungle was still again except for the braying of the mules and the groaning of wounded men among the corpses scattered all up and down the trail. Fargo looked around, gun still up; but there were no more targets. His eyes shuttled to the carts full of *stelae*; then he relaxed as he saw Nancy Telford, her father, and the man Norris raise their heads. But where was Stoneman?

Then he appeared, too, stepping around a cart, rifle in his hand. At his feet, a *pistolero* lay twitching with a belly wound. Stoneman put the gun muzzle against his head, pulled the trigger.

Fargo's mouth thinned. Yeah, he thought bitterly. That would be a job to his taste. Finishing off the wounded . . . All at once he was tired, a little shaky.

Then Nancy Telford had run to him. "Fargo! Are you all right?" She seized his arm. "Your face — "

"Just a bullet scratch."

"Thank God," she whispered. "I was afraid . . . !"

Down the trail, Stoneman's rifle went off again and then once more. Nancy dabbed at the bleeding cut on Fargo's cheek with a handkerchief and grimaced. "You know what he's doing?"

"Somebody has to. Let him. It's something he's good at."

"Yes." Her voice rasped. "Oh, I hate him. I don't know how I could ever have been such a fool. All he ever wanted of me anyhow was to use me to find out the hiding place of the cannon, bring us and his father together . . . Fargo — " Then she moved against him.

"All right," he said and put his arm around her, held her. "All right." Over her shoulder, he saw Stoneman staring at them, saw him half raise the rifle. Instinctively, Fargo stiffened, but Stoneman lowered the gun again.

Then Fargo released Nancy. "You go climb back on the cart. We've got no time to waste. We've got to move out again, right away."

"Yes." She looked at him a moment. "But . . . Fargo. Watch Ned. You hear? Watch Ned."

"I will," Fargo said. And he did, until Stoneman was back on the cart again and the wagon train rolled once more.

9

BELOW, Fargo could hear in darkness the river running. It was, he thought, a sound almost of salvation: the Belize, swollen by the autumn rains. They were in British Honduras now; and this was the river that would take them back to civilization, back to the capital of the country where Stoneman's yacht waited. Sitting in the darkness on the riverbank, shotgun cradled on his lap, he thought back over the past three weeks. He had made journeys in his time and taken risks, but never had he put in a harder, more dangerous twenty-one days than those just past.

He had scars and wounds to show for them: the marks of battle. They had fought their way all across the neck of Guatemala, between Chiapas and this British colony. First, after the ambush by the men from the *montería*, the *revolucionarios*; and they had been a different case entirely. Soldiers, well-armed, well-mounted, and they had swept down on the train in an open river valley where cover was scarce. But they had made one mistake; they had thought of the Golden Gun as loot, not artillery; and that had been their undoing. Its first charge had caught their bunched-up attack squarely with lethal force, mowing down men and horses in a ghastly pile. That had given Fargo, Darnley and the others the edge they needed for survival; but it had been a rough fight all the same. They had lost men, a lot of Darnley's Raiders and Norris, Telford's assistant, hit by a stray ricochet. The Mexicans had harassed them for miles before giving up. Almost before they were gone, the Guatemalan army came.

They were less difficult to deal with. Back country Indians given ill-fitting uniforms and obsolete rifles, they fought only because they feared their officers more than the enemy. They knew that even if they got the Golden Gun, they'd get no share of loot. Fargo and Darnley, with rifles, had concentrated on the leaders: the captain, the lieutenant and the non-coms. Expert snipers as they were, there seemed no hiding place from their bullets, and the one surviving sergeant had broken and run after seeing his superiors picked off by slugs that seemingly came from nowhere.

Then a skirmish with a tribe of poverty-stricken jungle Indians with obsolete muskets; the first thunder of the Golden Gun had put an end to that. Meanwhile, with all that fighting, the back-breaking labor of moving the loaded carts and the heavy cannon through jungle that was as much their enemy as the greedy, guntoting men who harassed them; and the jungle was an enemy unafraid of rifles, pistols, cannons; an enemy omnipresent and implacable, barring their way with brush and briars, sucking the wheels of the loaded carts and gun-carriage down into its bottomless mud, confronting them with flooded fords and swirling streams.

And yet, Fargo thought, they had beat them all: the bandits, the Indians, and the jungle. They had made it through this far. Tomorrow they would begin construction of rafts on which to float the carts and cannon down to the city of Belize.

In a sense, it was over. In another sense, Fargo knew, it was just beginning. Darnley. He still had to deal with Darnley. The English soldier of fortune was still determined to have the cannon, hold it for ransom from old Stoneman. Fargo had used him and he had used Fargo, and before they reached Belize there would have to be an accounting.

Fargo thought about that. Almost, he wished whatever it was within him that balked at going along with Darnley would dissolve and vanish. But he knew it would not; it was too much part of him. He made his living by jobs such as these; and the first time he doublecrossed a customer, that was it. When he hired out to do something and named a price, he did it — or was prepared to die in the trying. He had come close to dying this time; when Darnley finally learned that Fargo had used him, had no idea of holding back the Golden Gun from Stoneman, he might come closer.

But that was a matter for the future; and Fargo lived in the present, for the moment. Darnley's Raiders had been decimated in the fighting; only a handful were left. Probably he would let Darnley have the gun. Then he would raise more men in Belize and come back and take it from him. And yet, he hated to see the gun go to Stoneman.

Fargo loved weapons, as only a professional fighting man can. His love for a well-made, honest weapon was as strong as a lecher's love for women or a drunkard's lust for the bottle; strong as a cardsharp's love for the gambling thrill or a Kentuckian's madness over horses. And he had fallen in love with the Golden Gun. Not for the gold it contained, but because it was a fine weapon and it had served him well.

Stoneman, he thought bitterly, was not worthy of such a thing. But he was bound to get it for him and turn it over to him and he would.

Fargo tensed at a sound behind him in the darkness. Instantly, he was up and around, the shotgun leveled. Then he let out a long breath, recognizing the silhouette coming down the river bank. "Nancy," he said, lowering the Fox.

"Neal . . . " She came to him, moved into his arms. Her mouth found his, open, hungry . . . He felt the crush of her breasts against his chest.

The kiss lasted a long time. Two weeks ago, in the darkness, she had come to him the first time while he slept. He had awakened to find her in his bed, naked between his blankets. Always, he slept apart from the rest, and no one could hear them. He had taken what she had offered, needing it. And he had taken it time after time since then. Now he would take it again. It would be better this time because they were, for all practical purposes, out of danger.

Her hand moved across his back, stroking the hard muscles there, caressed his neck beneath his hairline. Her lower body shoved against him, pushing hard, greedily. Still holding each other, they moved into the brush beside the river. There they sank to the ground on a bed of foliage. They released each other; and then she was wriggling out of shirt and pants and he had unlatched his belt, and they came together once more, and the river's rush drowned out her panting, the moaning sound she made . . .

It was over. They lay together relaxed and motionless for a while; then Fargo lit a cigarette. "Neal," Nancy whispered. "We're almost to Belize. What then?"

He could not tell her about Darnley, the scheming and the fighting that still lay ahead. "I don't know."

"You'll come to Washington with us?"

"Maybe. I haven't been there in a long time."

"Oh, Neal, please, you must." Her nails dug into his shoulder.

"We'll see." He thought of Carla in that hotel room in Texas. They couldn't understand; none of them could understand. That for him there was always another mistress, another lover: risk, danger.

"Darling, you have to."

He sat up. "No, there's nothing I *have* to do. But . . . We'll talk about it in Belize. We . . . " He tensed. "Somebody's coming." Quickly, he passed her clothes. He himself was dressed in an instant, the shotgun in hand. He wriggled to the edge of brush, looked up river. He recognized the silhouette there: Stoneman. The man stood on the river's edge, looking downstream. He moved restlessly, almost as if he were watching, waiting for someone or something to come up the current. Fargo frowned.

Stoneman had been quiet, very quiet, ever since the ambush four days out of the Valley of Skulls. He had avoided Fargo and Nancy both, and made a fair gun in their fights, had otherwise behaved himself, kept to himself. Now that they had reached the river, he was suddenly restless.

"You go on back to camp the other way," Fargo whispered. "I'll be along directly."

"Yes." Nancy, fully dressed now, vanished into the brush. Fargo cautiously emerged into the open.

"Stoneman," he said.

Stoneman raised his head. "Fargo?"

"Yeah, it's me." Fargo walked up to him. "What are you looking for? Expecting somebody?"

Stoneman laughed shortly, contemptuously. "Yeah, Santa Claus."

Fargo stared at him a moment. "It's a long time 'til Christmas," he said finally.

"Maybe not as long as you think."

"What do you mean by that?"

"Nothing. Only. We're almost there, aren't we?"

"We're a long way from there yet. Keep your eyes open. There are Indians and jaguars in British Honduras, too." Thoughtfully, Fargo moved away, watching

Stoneman over his shoulder. Stoneman did not move; he only stood there, staring down the river.

Camp was in a clearing, where a huge fire blazed. What was left of Darnley's men, a pathetic remnant, sat around it — all except those posted on guard. In the flickering light, the Golden Gun gleamed dully, smeared with mud and travel-dirt. The single can of blasting powder and the last charge of rocks — there were none in this jungle — sat beneath its muzzle.

As Fargo entered the circle of firelight, Darnley got to his feet. The ordeal in the jungle had burnt off every ounce of surplus flesh; his clothes — what was left of them — hung like bags on his big frame. But the Colts in his holsters were spotless and well-oiled. "Everything quiet?" he asked.

"So far." Fargo was relieved to see that Nancy had made it back to camp safely; she stood by her father near the carts of *stelae*. Around the clearing, the *macheteros* and *arrieros* were already asleep in their hammocks. There were not many left of them, either. Some had been killed in the fighting. Two weeks before, three of them had deserted. Still, there were enough men left in camp to build the necessary rafts.

Fargo went to the Golden Gun; like a magnet, it seemed to draw him; it was hard for him to keep his hands off of it. He stroked the tube, tremendously heavy, satin soft. It had served him well, and he had served it well in turn. He had made it speak again after centuries of silence, and yet he had not destroyed it. It could have been destroyed, easily: gold was soft, even in as thick a mass as this tube. And the powerful modern giant powder he had been using as propellant for the charges of rocks was something it had never been designed to take. But he and the gun seemed part of one another; he knew what it could give and what it could take and he had never overcharged it nor fired it often enough to heat it and melt and flow it.

Darnley came to stand beside him,

feeling something of the same emotion. "Sweet piece, isn't it?" He patted the gun. "A real love."

"Yes," said Fargo.

"Stoneman will pay high for it," Darnley whispered. "We might go to a million and a quarter."

"Maybe." Fargo lit a cigarette. "It's not charged. I didn't charge it tonight."

"I know. Funny, it makes you feel almost naked, not having it loaded. Still, no reason for it, really. We'll have no trouble here we can't handle with small arms. And she's already taken a lot of stress; why push our luck?"

"That's the way I feel," Fargo said. "She's fired a lot of rounds she wasn't designed for." He turned away. "Guard detail set?"

"What there is of it. We're damned short of men. This sweet old girl has cost a lot of lives."

"I'll check them at midnight," Fargo said. "Now I'm going to get some sleep." He glanced at Nancy; their eyes met. Then he went to his hammock, well out of the circle of firelight. He unslung the shotgun, piled in, fully clad, drew blankets over his head to keep off mosquitoes. In two minutes, he was sound asleep, with the Colt by his side, his hand clasped around its grip.

When they took him, he never got a chance to use it.

He came out of sleep groggily, with something cold pressed against his forehead. Even before he opened his eyes, he knew it was a gun muzzle. His right hand came up instinctively, but it was pinned, another hand, just as strong as his, ripped the colt from it. Then a cold voice said, "Don't move. You understand? Don't move."

Fargo lay rigidly. All he could see was the blackness of two figures in darkness. One held a pistol against his head, between the eyes. "Who're you?" he managed.

"No bloody business of yours." The gun barrel came away. "Up and out, damned easy. Otherwise, you're dead."

He was not fool enough to buck that kind of drop. He lifted himself out of the hammock, stood up. Usually, he slept like an animal, ready to go into action at the faintest sound, but the ordeal of the jungle trip had exhausted him. And so they — whoever they were — had taken him as if he were a child. He cursed silently as strong hands frisked him, whisked away the Batangas knife. Then he was roughly turned around. "March!" a voice said. "Over to the fire!"

In the center of the clearing, it blazed high. Men were grouped around it, and they held guns. They were not Darnley's men. Fargo strode into the opening with a pistol probing at his spine. Then he halted.

He had expected anything: but he had not expected this.

Ned Stoneman sat beside the fire in a camp chair. Not young Ned Stoneman, but the old one, the withered man who was his father. He sat there with a pistol in his lap, and the light glinted on the cold blue eyes in the drawn face. His puckered mouth twisted in what might have been a smile as Fargo was pushed up to stand beside a disarmed Darnley, Telford, and Nancy.

And young Ned Stoneman stood behind the chair, Fargo's own shotgun trained on the group.

"Hello, Fargo," old Stoneman said, his voice still like the crackling of dry leaves. "Surprised to see me?"

"Maybe."

"I still had one last journey left in me." The old man got to his feet unsteadily. He moved to the Golden Gun, leaned against it for support. "Ned sent word to Belize by three Indians he bribed to desert you. That you had got the Golden Gun and were on your way. I was on my yacht there; it had come and picked me up." The clawlike hand stroked the golden tube as if it were womanflesh. "I couldn't rest, you see. I was afraid. Afraid that something would happen. That I would never touch this Golden Gun, never own it, never possess it. So when the Indians came with Ned's message, I got some men together. We came up the river in canoes. A hard journey for a man my age, but — " still stroking the cannon of pure gold " — well worth it."

He laughed, a croaking sound. "We took out what few, tired guards you had posted without making any noise. Now we've got you. And the cannon. You and Darnley, of course — I know his reputation. When I heard he was with you, I understood everything — the two of you had planned to doublecross me."

"No," Fargo said. "No, I was going to bring the gun to you."

Darnley whirled, looked at him. "You'd have had to kill me first!"

"I was prepared for that, too," Fargo said quickly. "I was going to keep my bargain, Stoneman."

"Then you're a fool," Stoneman said. "Enough gold to make you rich for the rest of your life, and you were going to deliver it for a lousy forty thousand? You expect me to believe that?"

Fargo was silent.

"That's right," said Stoneman. "It doesn't matter what I believe. Since you'll all be dead in a few minutes anyhow."

"All?" Fargo rasped. He looked at Telford, Nancy.

Stoneman's mouth warped in his ghastly smile. In the firelight he was like a mummy leaning on the cannon, his son behind him with leveled sawed-off. "All," he said. "I hate to deprive the world of a scientist like Dr. Telford, but I have no choice. I led him to believe the Golden Gun and his *stelae* would go to the Smithsonian. Actually, all — all, do you understand? — go to my collection. The *stelae* will complete it, and this . . . this is the realization of my youthful dream . . . " He stroked the barrel again. "Besides, Ned has a score to settle with Nancy, poor girl. And you can't expect Dr. Telford to keep silent about the murder of his daughter."

He paused, as if so much talking had exhausted his strength. "Anyhow, you're alone now, all of you. Darnley's Raiders are finished. We've cut a lot of throats tonight . . . "

Darnley tensed. "You've — ?"

"We killed them quietly," Stoneman said. "All of them."

Darnley made a sound in his throat. Then, quite without warning he threw himself at Stoneman. "You bastard!" he howled.

Stoneman raised the pistol in his hand and pulled the trigger. The bullet caught Darnley between the eyes, and the big Englishman fell forward into the coals at the edge of the fire.

"That ends Darnley and his Raiders," Stoneman said. "Now, Fargo, you see how I operate? In my younger days down here, I made you look like a Sunday School superintendent. That's how a man gets rich, Fargo — rich and powerful. You have to be prepared to stop at nothing, break any bargain, violate any deal . . . " He coughed dryly. "I've talked too much." He hawked, spat phlegm. "This gun. Since I first heard of it, decades ago, I've dreamed of it, dreamed of hearing it speak. You've used it, Fargo, used it to kill men after hundreds of years."

Fargo stood tensely.

"Before it goes silent once again — perhaps forever — I want to hear it talk," Stoneman said.

"Mr. Stoneman — !" Telford burst out furiously. But ten men were ranged behind the old man and five more held guns on Telford, his daughter, and on Fargo.

"I was an artilleryman once," said Stoneman. "Years ago, in the Union army. I know such guns. And Ned has described to me how you've used it. And so, now . . . stand close together, all of you. Don't move, or, I assure you, you'll be shot. Not fatally, but enough to disable you. Even the girl. Then you'll die slowly instead of swiftly. Ned. If you will . . . "

"You're damned right," said his son. He laid the shotgun across the camp chair, went to the cannon. He opened the can of blasting powder, poured some down the tube of the Golden Gun.

His father watched him closely. "Not too much. Gold doesn't have the tensile strength of steel. That's enough."

"All right," young Ned said. "Sure." But he gave the canister another shake before he lowered it. His face was savage as he crammed in wadding. Fargo watched closely, standing rigidly, as Ned pounded the cloth home fiercely. Then he poured in sharp, jagged rocks, a whole load.

"Be careful," Stoneman said. "Don't give it more than it can handle."

"I told you, I've seen Fargo do it a dozen times."

"Yes, but — "

Ned rammed home more wadding. He went behind the gun, leveled it and turned its trail. Now the dark Cyclopean eye of its bore was centered on Fargo, who stood between Nancy and her father.

Ned squinted along the barrel as he'd seen Fargo do, then straightened up. He sliced a piece of fuse, rammed it down the touch hole. "It's ready," he said. He took a match from his pocket and handed it to his father.

"Thank you," the old man said. He moved with shambling steps to the gun's breech. Ned stepped aside.

"Just one more time. To hear this weapon speak, to let it drink blood. In my presence." The old man's eyes glittered in the firelight. He struck the match, touched it to the fuse. Fargo saw the tiny stars of sparks as the fuse caught and burned. Then he struck out on either side with terrific blows that knocked Nancy and her father sprawling, and in the same moment he fell forward on his face and began to roll.

Suddenly it was if all the world had blown sky-high. A sheet of flame filled the clearing, the sound of the cannon skull-crushing in its intensity, its thundering roar. The very earth vibrated and men screamed, and Fargo heard the fluttering *whoosh* of rocks above his head and leaped to his feet and ran to the camp chair and seized his loaded shotgun. Three men charged at him in a group and he loosed the right barrel, pointed high, and he shot all three in their faces. The clearing was rank with the smell of powder, blood and torn flesh, the old familiar smells of combat, and even with his ears ringing and brain shaking from the massive explosion, Fargo was in his element, armed, fighting, doing what he, like the bronze cock in San Antonio, had been bred and born to do. He threw himself forward across the three men he had killed and scooped up a pistol as he did so. Then he came up with the shotgun in one hand and a Colt in the other and for the first time he saw what had happened.

There was nothing left of the Golden Gun but a riven chunk of smoking gold on a destroyed, sagging carriage. Blood dripped from its golden tube, and except for that, nothing remained of old Ned Stoneman, caught in the explosion of the breech. That extra shake of powder, that hard tamping of wadding, that savage overload of rocks — it was more than the old, soft, precious gun could take. It had blown up like a bomb, and it had taken old Stoneman and half his men with it.

Then gunfire rattled; Telford, on his knees, had seized a Winchester blown clear by the explosion. He was using it, and Fargo saw men fall. Fargo scrambled to his feet and a gun flared from the outer edge of darkness. He punched a shot at the flame with the pistol in his hand and heard a man scream, and then somebody called his name. "Fargo! Goddamn you, Fargo!" And he whirled, and there across the fire was young Ned Stoneman. He had a pistol lined on Fargo, and his finger pulled the trigger.

Fargo fired the other shotgun barrel, without aiming. At the same moment, he fell sideways again.

There was no need to aim, only point. Those nine spreading slugs snapped across the blazing fire and most of them took young Stoneman in the head and chest. His upper body seemed to dissolve, his shot went wild; he staggered backward under the impact. Then, miraculously, what was left of him, by pure, reflexive nervous action, caught its balance and came upright. It stood there, nearly headless, spouting blood. Then it fell forward across the flames.

Fargo came up with his handgun ready.

But there was no more gunfire. Only the hissing of the campfire flames, the smell of burning flesh, and the rank fumes of cordite. Crouching, he turned in a cull circle. Then he stood up straight.

Nancy began to scream — loudly, with hysteria.

"It's all right," her father said. "Honey, it's all right. They're dead. They're all dead."

10

THE Governor of British Honduras was a thick-bodied pompous man with a red mustache. Behind his desk he leaned back in his chair and snorted, and the mustache riffled.

"A preposterous story." He looked from Fargo to Telford to Nancy Telford with pale green eyes. "Do you think I can accept it? Here I have on my hands an international incident; the most powerful man in the United States leaves his yacht at Belize, goes up-country, and he and his son disappear. And you tell me that they died in an accidental explosion up the headwaters of the Belize. And do you think the United States will believe that? With an adventurer, a soldier of fortune, like yourself mixed up in it?"

Fargo took out a thin, black cigar, clamped it between his teeth, lit it. He itched, but he did not scratch. Even

222

the jails of British Honduras, like all those in this part of the world, were full of fleas. He had spent enough time in the Belize prison to acquire his quota of flea-bites. "You've had the story," he said. "We brought out the Mayan *stelae*. Mr. Stoneman came upriver to meet us . . . and his son. We used blasting powder to fell trees to make rafts and unfortunately, both Stonemans got caught in a misfire."

"Oh, of course. And so you appear on the scene with hundreds of pounds of jagged lumps of pure gold, which we are supposed to presume you — what? Mined on the Belize? Which we have impounded. And — " He broke off. "Tell me. If you will only tell me the real story. Look, Fargo, Darnley's Raiders were a thorn in our side. They're all gone now, and that's to your advantage. But I can't just confront the American government with a cock-and-bull story about the disappearance of one of the richest, most powerful citizens of America and his son. I know the Mayan *stelae* you've brought

223

out are valuable beyond compare. Those I'm prepared to release to the Smithsonian in Washington. But the gold? and the death of Stoneman? Fargo, can I release to you a half-ton of pure gold and let you go without knowing the truth of the death of Stoneman?"

"You have heard all I'm gonna say," Fargo told him. "As a matter of fact, if there's any more, you're better off not knowing it."

"Just the same — " The Governor broke off as someone knocked on the double mahogany doors of his chambers. "Come in," he grunted.

"Sir." The aide, a British Navy ensign, saluted briskly. "This signal, from His Majesty's cruiser *Norfolk*." He thrust over a folded square of paper.

The Governor unwrapped it, read it. Fargo saw his florid face change. Then he hitched his bulk up in his chair and sighed. "Apparently I underestimated you, Mr. Fargo. It seems you have friends in high places." He read aloud: "*Release Fargo and all personal possessions,*

whatever they might be. Strong represen-
tations from high American authorities,
especially past President Roosevelt, make
this imperative. Stoneman under indictment
for violation anti-trust laws in oil and
railroads; presumed disappeared to avoid
investigation. Tender all possible help
Fargo and Telford's passage to Washington."

The Governor laid down the square of paper. "Signed by the King of England. Not the Foreign Secretary, not the Colonial Secretary, not the Prime Minister. His Majesty himself."

Fargo let his wolf's grin go. His single message to the ex-Colonel of the Rough Riders had borne satisfactory fruit.

"So the case is closed unless your own government wishes to reopen it. Very well, I understand the *Norfolk* is bound north. I trust that will be satisfactory transportation."

Fargo's grin widened. "Very," he said, with vast relief.

In the room on the cruiser he had been assigned to, he opened the crudely made tarpaulin bag. It had taken a crane to haul it aboard. Within it, the jagged remnants of what had been the Golden Gun glittered at him dully.

Fargo looked down at them with a certain sadness. The blast had scattered golden hunks like shrapnel far and wide; he had retrieved this much. It was worth a fortune, maybe the biggest score he had ever made until now. A quarter of a million dollars, likely . . . then he looked up as his stateroom door opened.

Nancy Telford stood there.

"May I come in?" she asked, almost shyly.

"Yeah," said Fargo.

She entered. She looked at the vast pile of wracked, golden metal. "What will you do with all that money?"

"Drink some of it up, gamble some of it away . . . "

"All that?" Her voice rose. "You could live forever on so much — "

"No," Fargo said. "Nobody lives forever."

She looked at him.

"Especially not me," he said.

"Neal." She came to him, put a hand on his. "There's a fortune there. All you have to do is settle down, enjoy it . . . "

"And rot away."

"Not with someone you love and who loved you to see to you."

Fargo took out a cigarette, lit it. "And get old. Let the kidneys go, the liver and the lungs. Fall apart inside, while I rock on my front porch and sip my soup."

"You make it sound so awful."

He grinned. "It's all right for those who like it." Then he stood up. "It's more than I can spend before I'll be ready for another job. I'd thought about donating part of it to a worthy cause."

Nancy looked at him. "What?"

"The rest of the *stelae* there in the Valley of Skulls. When the revolution's over, somebody ought to go there and bring them out. I figured that since your daddy originated the whole idea and nursed everything along, maybe half of this ought to go to him for that."

Her eyes widened. "Fargo."

"What the hell," he said. "One man

can only spend so much money. That's what Stoneman couldn't get through his head."

She stood there motionless. Then she said, "He'll be so relieved, so delighted — " She raised her face, looked at him with eyes of lambent green. "But . . . how long will you be in Washington?"

"Longer than I figured," Fargo said. "There'll be an investigation, I know that; I'll be tied up for a while."

Her breasts rose and fell. "Good. The longer the better."

"I was thinking the same thing," Fargo said. "We'll have a spell together, anyhow."

Her lips moved soundlessly, forming the words *Thank God*. Her eyes met his.

"If we'll be together so long," she said, "maybe we'd better get in practice."

"You know," said Fargo, "I was thinking that, too." He threw the tarp over the remnants of the Golden Gun and reached for her, pulling her to him . . .

BRETT RANDALL, GAMBLER
E. B. Mann

Larry Day had the choice of running away from the law or of assuming a dead man's place. No matter what he decided he was bound to end up dead.

THE GUNSHARP
William R. Cox

The Eggerleys weren't very smart. They trained their sights on Will Carney and Arizona's biggest blood bath began.

THE DEPUTY OF SAN RIANO
Lawrence A. Keating and
Al. P. Nelson

When a man fell dead from his horse, Ed Grant was spotted riding away from the scene. The deputy sheriff rode out after him and came up against everything from gunfire to dynamite.

HELL RIDERS
Steve Mensing

Wade Walker's kid brother, Duane, was locked up in the Silver City jail facing a rope at dawn. Wade was a ruthless outlaw, but he was smart, and he had vowed to have his brother out of jail before morning!

DESERT OF THE DAMNED
Nelson Nye

The law was after him for the murder of a marshal — a murder he didn't commit. Breen was after him for revenge — and Breen wouldn't stop at anything . . . blackmail, a frameup . . . or murder.

DAY OF THE COMANCHEROS
Steven C. Lawrence

Their very name struck terror into men's hearts — the Comancheros, a savage army of cutthroats who swept across Texas, leaving behind a blood-stained trail of robbery and murder.

SUNDANCE: SILENT ENEMY
John Benteen

A lone crazed Cheyenne was on a personal war path. They needed to pit one man against one crazed Indian. That man was Sundance.

LASSITER
Jack Slade

Lassiter wasn't the kind of man to listen to reason. Cross him once and he'll hold a grudge for years to come — if he let you live that long.

LAST STAGE TO GOMORRAH
Barry Cord

Jeff Carter, tough ex-riverboat gambler, now had himself a horse ranch that kept him free from gunfights and card games. Until Sturvesant of Wells Fargo showed up.

WOLF DOG RANGE
Lee Floren

Will Ardery would stop at nothing, unless something stopped him first — like a bullet from Pete Manly's gun.

DEVIL'S DINERO
Marshall Grover

Plagued by remorse, a rich old reprobate hired the Texas Troubleshooters to deliver a fortune in greenbacks to each of his victims.

GUNS OF FURY
Ernest Haycox

Dane Starr, alias Dan Smith, wanted to close the door on his past and hang up his guns, but people wouldn't let him.

RIFLES ON THE RANGE
Lee Floren

Doc Mike and the farmer stood there alone between Smith and Watson. There was this moment of stillness, and then the roar would start. And somebody would die . . .

HARTIGAN
Marshall Grover

Hartigan had come to Cornerstone to die. He chose the time and the place, and Main Street became a battlefield.

SUNDANCE: OVERKILL
John Benteen

When a wealthy banker's daughter was kidnapped by the Cheyenne, he offered Sundance $10,000 to rescue the girl.